"Nothing's changed."

"You can't say that," Bernardo said flatly. "Everything has changed."

Angie tried to turn away but he took hold of her shoulders and kept her facing him. If she'd have shown the slightest sign of softening, he would have drawn her into his arms and kissed her ardently. And then, even he, who was uneasy with words, would have tried to tell her of the bittersweet happiness that had possessed him ever since he'd suspected that she was to bear his child. He was an old-fashioned man and, above all, a Sicilian. To create a child with a beloved woman was a joy that wiped out all else.

He stared at her. "The sooner our marriage takes place, the better."

"Us? Get married?" she echoed. "Why would we do that?"

He was floundering again. Angie's eyes were full of a cool appraisal that baffled him. "Because we are having a baby," he said.

Dear Reader,

Being married to an Italian, I take a special delight in writing about Italian men—the most fascinating and endearing men on earth. I've enjoyed telling the stories of the three Martelli brothers.

Although linked by kinship, they are all different. Lorenzo, the youngest, is a merry charmer. Renato, the eldest, is head of the family, a man of confidence and power. Bernardo is their half brother. Only part of him belongs to the family. The other part is a loner who finds it hard to accept love.

And then there is Sicily, their home, one of the most beautiful places on earth, where people's true passions rise to the surface, giving them the courage to follow their hearts.

Husband by Necessity is the story of Bernardo—who has to fight for that courage after nearly throwing away the love of his life—and Angie, a remarkable woman who dares everything to lead him into the light.

With best wishes,

Lucy Gordon

HUSBAND BY NECESSITY

Lucy Gordon

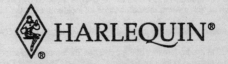

TORONTO • NEW YORK • LONDON
AMSTERDAM • PARIS • SYDNEY • HAMBURG
STOCKHOLM • ATHENS • TOKYO • MILAN • MADRID
PRAGUE • WARSAW • BUDAPEST • AUCKLAND

ISBN 0-373-03659-0

HUSBAND BY NECESSITY

First North American Publication 2001.

Copyright © 2001 by Lucy Gordon.

This edition published by arrangement with Harlequin Books S.A.

® and TM are trademarks of the publisher. Trademarks indicated with
® are registered in the United States Patent and Trademark Office, the
Canadian Trade Marks Office and in other countries.

Visit us at www.eHarlequin.com

Printed in U.S.A.

CHAPTER ONE

'ANGIE,' Heather called, not for the first time, 'the cab's here.'

'I'm ready,' Angie called back, not entirely truthfully. She *would* be ready when she'd finished applying her eye make-up and just touched her lips. It was an article of faith with her not to travel unless looking her best, even when time was fast running out.

For ten minutes the cab had been standing in a down-pour outside the London house that the two young women shared. The driver had hauled the last of the luggage down the steps, leaving only Heather, standing by the door, frantically calling back into the house,

'Angie, the cab!'

'I know, I know,' Angie called back. 'You told me.'

'I *know* I told you. I told you ages ago and you haven't moved.'

'Coming, coming, coming,' Angie muttered frantically to herself. 'Have I got everything? Well, if I haven't, it can't be helped. Any minute now, she's going to kill me.' She raised her voice and called back to Heather. 'Tell the man to take the bags out.'

Heather sounded as though she were dancing with frustration. 'He's already done that. Angie, I'm going to Sicily to get married, and if you don't mind I'd prefer to get there *before* the wedding.'

'But that's not for a week, is it?' Angie asked, appearing at that moment.

'Well, I'd like not to cut it too fine, and that includes not missing the plane.'

It was the perfect day for leaving London. The rain poured down in buckets, making the journey from the front door to the cab a mad dash. The two young women made it, laughing with delight at escaping, at being on their way to the sun, laughing because they were young and happy and one of them was getting married; because life was good despite the rain.

'Look at that!' Angie said when the door was shut behind them. 'Have you ever seen such rain? Oh, it's good to be going.' She saw her friend eyeing her askance and added penitently, 'Sorry I kept you waiting.'

'I don't know how you ever got to be a doctor,' Heather said. 'You're the most disorganised person I know.'

'Ah, but I'm not a disorganised doctor,' Angie said with truth. 'It's just that in my private life I tended to be—you know.'

'Birdbrained, scatty and infuriating,' Heather said.

Angie stretched happily. 'I really need a holiday. I'm worn out.'

'I should think you are. It must be tiring running away from all your admirers, Bill and Steve and—'

'Bill and Steve?' Angie looked aghast.

'You do remember them don't you?'

'Oh, yes. Last month. History.'

'Do they know they're history?' Heather asked.

'I tried to break it to them gently,' Angie said. She added, with a touch of wounded innocence, 'I always do.'

'So who was that man who came by last night begging you to come back soon?'

'That was George—I think.'

Heather chuckled. 'Honestly Angie, you're incorrigible.'

'No I'm not. I'm extremely corrigible—whatever that means. Anyway, I need a holiday because I've been working so hard. Accident and Emergency is exhausting enough, but when it's night duty as well—' She mopped her brow and looked plaintive.

They had shared a house in London for six years. Heather was quietly lovely and her nature was reserved and modest. The attraction of opposites had decreed that her dearest friend should be Angie, a radiant social butterfly who seemed to regard the world of men as provided for her personal entertainment.

At this moment she was contemplating the pleasures to come. 'Sunshine, sparkling blue sea, miles of golden sand, and lots of gorgeous Sicilian young men, all liberally endowed with S.A. Or at the very least, C.H.'

Angie divided male attractiveness into two categories— S.A., sex appeal, and C.H., come hither. As far as Heather could understand her friend's marking system, S.A. was the more immediately exciting, while C.H. was the more subtle and intriguing. Since Angie was, herself, liberally endowed with both qualities, she was in a good position to judge.

'You make C.H. sound like the poor relation,' Heather objected now.

'Not really. But it takes time, and I don't have time. S.A. is better for short stretches.'

'Well, you behave yourself.'

'No way,' Angie said at once. 'I don't come on holiday to behave myself. I come to get a sun tan, fall in love, sample the local delights and act *outrageously*. Otherwise what's the point?'

It was easy to believe that she meant every word. Angie was daintily built, barely five foot three, with blonde hair and deep blue eyes. Her nature was romantic and impulsive. She became easily infatuated and, since she looked, according to one besotted admirer, 'Like the fairy on the Christmas tree,' she had no trouble inspiring infatuation in return. The result had been a string of intense, short-lived relationships which had caused Heather to describe Angie as a serial flirt.

But appearances were deceptive. Dr Angela Wendham's love affairs were brief because her true, enduring love was her work. Her ethereal look concealed a brain that had carried her through medical school with honours. She'd gone on to four exhausting years postgraduate training, including stints in Accident and Emergency departments, coping not merely with casualties but with drunks and vicious louts. She was skilled at dealing with both kinds of crises.

But now she planned only to enjoy herself. Heather was about to marry Lorenzo Martelli, a young Sicilian. Angie was to be the bridesmaid, and since it was her first real holiday since she-couldn't-remember-when, she was going to make the most of it.

It was still raining when they reached the airport. They got quickly into the main hall, pushing a trolley piled high with bags, most of which were Angie's. Her petite figure and striking beauty repaid good dressing, and she happily gave them their due.

As they were waiting to check in there was a strangled cry of, 'Angie!' from the crowd, and a damp young man appeared beside them. In his hand he bore one perfect red rose.

'I couldn't let you go without saying goodbye,' he said soulfully, offering it to her. 'You won't forget me, will you?'

'Of course I won't,' Angie said, deeply moved. 'Oh, Fred—'

'Frank,' the young man said edgily.

'Frank, you'll be in my thoughts every moment I'm away.'

Frank seized her hand and kissed it. Luckily they reached the head of the queue and in the check-in formalities he was forced to retreat. Angie couldn't meet her friend's eye.

'The sooner I get you safely out of the country the better,' Heather said with feeling.

It was raining even harder as their plane took off, climbing into the clouds. But then they broke through into light, and they both pressed eagerly against the window until the air hostess brought them a snack.

'I can't get my head around you being swept off your feet,' Angie told Heather. 'Much more my crazy style than yours.'

'Yes, it's not like sturdy, dependable me, is it?' Heather mused. 'Dashing off to live in another country, practically another world.'

Angie was diplomatically silent but she couldn't help wondering about Peter who had been Heather's fiancé for a year before dumping her a week before the wedding.

'I'm not on the rebound,' Heather said, reading her unspoken thoughts. 'I love Lorenzo, and we're going to make a wonderful life together in Sicily.'

'You're right. New horizons. Lovely.' Angie's face assumed a look in which mischief and innocence were evenly matched. 'You did say Lorenzo had two brothers, didn't you?'

'I've only met one of them, Renato.'

'Yes, you told me. I can't believe that any man would behave like that, actually coming to your counter at Gossways, pretending to be a customer, just so that he could look you up and down.'

Gossways was the most luxurious department store in London, and Heather had been working there, selling perfumes.

'I don't blame him for wanting to meet the woman his brother was courting,' Heather said now. 'It's just the way he did it. Not a hint about who he was, and then, when Lorenzo took me to meet him at the Ritz that night, there he sat, just waiting for me to walk into his lair.'

The meeting had been dramatic. Renato Martelli had approved of Heather, but in such a high-handed manner that she'd stormed out of the Ritz, nearly killing both of them under the wheels of a taxi. In the high drama of that evening Lorenzo had begged her to marry him, and she had relented. Now, barely a month later, she was on her way to Sicily for the marriage. She had, as Angie said, been swept off her feet.

'Tell me about the other brother,' Angie said now.

'His name's Bernardo, and he's their half-brother. Their father had an affair with a woman from one of the mountain villages, called Marta Tornese, and Bernardo was their son. They died together in a car crash, and Lorenzo's mother took the boy in and raised him with her own sons.'

'My goodness! What a woman!'

The plane was banking, showing them the triangular island of Sicily, golden and beautiful against the blue of the sea. In another moment they had started the final descent to Palermo Airport.

As they came out of Customs, Heather broke into a smile and waved at two men standing apart. From Heather's description Angie knew that the glamorous young giant with light brown curly hair was Lorenzo, her friend's fiancé. She glanced at the other and felt a smile begin deep inside her.

He wasn't a tall man, something which the petite Angie

greatly appreciated. She hated getting a crick in her neck. So it was a mark in his favour that he was only five foot eight. His shape earned him a good review too. Ten out of ten, she thought, for lean wiriness, narrow hips and a look of hard, compact maleness that sent an uncompromising message to the woman who knew how to read it.

So far, so enjoyable.

It was when she got closer and saw his dark, serious eyes that her inner smile faltered a little. There was something about this man that she couldn't smile at, something that sent a shiver of excited anticipation up her spine.

As Heather and Lorenzo threw themselves into each other's arms the young man approached Angie, smiling very slightly. 'I am Bernardo Tornese,' he said in a deep voice.

Tornese, she noticed, not Martelli.

She took the hand he was holding out, and felt the whipcord strength of him, even in that light grip. 'I'm Angela Wendham,' she said.

'It is a great pleasure to meet you, Signorina Wendham.'

She could have listened to his voice forever. It was dark, resonant and beautiful. 'Just Angie,' she said, smiling.

'Angie, I am very glad to meet you.'

She sensed that he was studying her, just as she was doing with him. That was fine. She knew she didn't have to fear being looked at, even when she'd just got off a plane.

The lovers had finished their greeting and disentangled themselves, a little self-consciously. Heather introduced Angie to her future husband, who then said, 'This is my brother, Bernardo.'

'Half-brother,' murmured Bernardo at once.

The drive to the Martelli house just outside Palermo took half an hour. There was so much beauty about Sicily to be taken in that Angie became dazed by the profusion. The hot streets of Palermo soon gave way to the country-side with its riot of flowers and the gleaming blue sea that came more into view as they climbed higher. At last a great three-storied building came into sight, and Lorenzo, from the back seat, called, 'There it is.'

The Residenza stood on an incline overlooking the sea. It was a magnificent mediaeval edifice of yellow stone. In their own way the Martellis were princes and they lived appropriately.

'That's your home?' Angie gasped.

'That's the Residenza Martelli,' Bernardo replied. He was concentrating on the road, and didn't seem aware of the quick look Angie gave him.

A moment later they had swung into the courtyard, and there was Baptista Martelli just emerging onto the great steps to wait for them. She was a small, frail-looking woman in her sixties, who looked as though life had aged her prematurely. Her hair was white and her face deli-cately beautiful. Angie regarded her with interest as Heather's future mother in law, but she was also fasci-nated to know what kind of a woman took in her hus-band's illegitimate offspring and reared him with her own sons. Baptista greeted her warmly, although Angie couldn't help reading the message in her eyes.

A will of steel, she thought. *She'll cover it with charm, but it will always be there.*

But then Baptista smiled at her, and her sharp eyes softened to warmth.

A dangerous enemy, Angie thought, *but a wonderful friend.*

She noticed the exuberant hug Lorenzo gave his

mother, while Bernardo contented himself with a peck on the cheek. His behaviour was faultless, yet the manner was courteous rather than loving.

A maid was detailed to show the two young women to the bedroom they were to share, and then bring them to the terrace where Baptista would be waiting for them with refreshments.

Their room had two large four-poster beds, hung with white net curtains. More net curtains hung at the floor-length windows that led out onto the broad terrace over-looking a magnificent garden. Angie, who was a demon gardener when she could get the time, promised herself a leisurely exploration of that garden. Beyond it the land stretched away, reaching to dark, misty mountains on the horizon.

The maid was unpacking their cases. Angie hurriedly changed out of the serviceable jeans she'd worn for trav-elling, into a light, floaty dress of a blue that turned her eyes to violet. When they were both ready the maid led them out onto the terrace and round to the front of the house where Baptista was seated at a small rustic table, laden with refreshments. Bernardo and Lorenzo were also there, handing them to their seats and filling their glasses with Marsala.

'May I get you something to eat?' Bernardo enquired, indicating the candied fruit ring, zabaglione, Sicilian cheesecake and coffee ice with whipped cream.

'My goodness,' Angie said faintly.

'Baptista is the world's greatest hostess,' he said. 'When she doesn't know what her guests will like, she orders everything, just in case.'

'Baptista', Angie noticed. Not 'my mother'. She re-membered how quickly he'd said 'half-brother' at the air-port, and for a moment she felt a frisson in the air. Her

instincts were telling her that this was a complicated man
who carried his own tensions everywhere. She felt her
curiosity rising.

He helped her to food and wine, and gently asked if
she had everything she needed, but he took little part in
the general conversation. Angie thought she would never
have known him to be a brother of Lorenzo, about whom
so much was light, from his curly hair to his smile.
Everything about Bernardo was dark. His skin had the
weather beaten swarthiness of a man who lived amongst
the elements. His eyes were so dark they seemed almost
black, and his hair was truly black.

His face intrigued her. When in repose it had a set,
rock-like quality. His eyes were deep set and full of secrets, his mouth slightly heavy. But it became mobile and
changeable as soon as he spoke, and animation glowed
from him.

At last Baptista indicated that she would like to be left
alone with Heather. Lorenzo slipped away and Bernardo
turned to Angie. 'May I show you the gardens?' he asked.

'I should love that,' she said happily, taking the hand
he offered.

The great garden of the Residenza was a show place,
tended by a dozen gardeners. At its centre was a large
stone fountain featuring mythical beasts spouting water in
all directions. From this relayed a dozen paths, some wandering past flower beds, others curving mysteriously into
the trees. Bernardo conscientiously pointed out every va-
riety of plant, and she had the feeling that he had learned
them as a duty. It was as though this magnificent place
forced him to be something he wasn't. Angie's curiosity
increased.

'Have you and Heather known each other very long?'
he asked.

'About six years. She had a job in a paper shop just around the corner from where I was doing my medical training.'

'Ah, you're a nurse?'

'I'm a doctor,' Angie said, slightly nettled at his assumption.

'Forgive me,' he said hastily. 'Sicily is still a little old-fashioned in some respects.'

'Evidently.'

They walked side by side for a few minutes. 'Are you annoyed with me?' he asked at last.

'No,' she said too quickly.

'I think you are. Try not to be. I spend my life in the mountains where people still hark back to an earlier age. To you, perhaps, we would appear rough and uncivilised.'

He didn't smile, but there was a gentleness in his manner that won her over. Her curiosity about him was growing.

'I'm not annoyed,' she said. 'It was silly of me to make a fuss about nothing. I was telling you about Heather. We got to know and like each other, and eventually moved in together. We've shared a home for several years now.'

'Can you tell me something about her? She's so different from—that is, Lorenzo—' He stopped in some confusion.

It was odd, she thought, that this man from a wealthy background should seem so shy and ill at ease. Whatever else he might be, he wasn't a smooth-tongued charmer, and she liked him better for it.

'Lorenzo has played the field with ladies of easy virtue and you're wondering what Heather is like,' she supplied cheerfully.

Bernardo coloured and pulled himself together. 'Since Renato approves of her I know she's not a lady of easy virtue,' he said hastily. 'He speaks of her in the highest terms.'

'She doesn't speak of *him* in the highest terms,' Angie said darkly. 'She says he behaved outrageously.'

'Yes, I've heard the story about that evening. I think those two will always be at odds, with Lorenzo in the middle, being pulled each way.'

'I'm interested to meet Renato. What's he like?'

'He's the head of the family,' Bernardo said with a hint of austerity in his tone.

'And that really means something here, I guess.'

'Doesn't it mean something in your country?'

'Not really,' Angie said, considering. 'Of course, we all respect my father, but that's because he's been a doctor for forty years and helped thousands of people.'

'Is that why you became a doctor too?'

'We all did, my two brothers and me. And my mother was a doctor when she was alive. She died while I was still doing my training.'

'Then your parents founded a dynasty.'

Angie laughed. 'I wish Dad could hear you. He never encouraged us to follow his footsteps. I remember him saying, "Whatever you do, don't go into medicine. It's a dog's life and you won't get any sleep for years." Of course, we all did. But I must tell you—' she eyed Bernardo mischievously, 'that in England a man doesn't get respect just for being a man. In fact—'

'Go on,' Bernardo said with a smile far back in his dark eyes. 'You are longing to say something that will be "one in the eye" for me.'

'When I took my medical exams, it was a point of honour with me to get higher marks than either of my brothers. I did too.' She giggled as gleefully as a child. 'They were *so mad*.'

The smile had reached Bernardo's mouth. He was regarding her with delight. 'And your Papa?'

'Before the exams he said, "Go for it!" and afterwards he said, "Good on you!"'

'And what did your brothers say?'

'Before or after they'd put arsenic in my soup? They just doubled up with laughter at the thought of what I had in front of me.'

'And what was that?'

'Four years of post-graduate work. General medicine, general surgery, accident and emergency, obstetrics, gynaecology, paediatrics, psychiatry and general practice.'

'It sounds terrible,' Bernardo said, half laughing, half frowning.

'It was. I think it's made as nightmarish as possible to discourage the weaklings. But I'm no weakling. Look at that.' She clenched her fist and bent her arm in a 'Mr Muscleman' pose.

Bernardo laid tentative fingers on the barely perceptible bulge. 'I'm terrified,' he said with a smile. 'All these qualifications, and you're only—' he regarded her warily. He'd been going to say 'only a little girl' but decided hastily against it.

'I'm twenty-eight years old,' she declared, 'and a lot tougher than I look.'

'You could scarcely be less,' Bernardo observed, with an admiring glance at her fairy figure.

She laughed and ran a few steps ahead of him to where the path vanished into a tunnel of trees, and turned, skipping backwards, teasing him. As holiday romances went, this one showed signs of going very well. He didn't run after her as another man might have done, but simply held out his hand, watching her, until she stopped skipping and laid her fingers lightly in his palm.

Hand in hand they strolled among the trees, while a sense of enchantment crept over her. It was nothing he said or did. He wasn't the most handsome man in the world. He wasn't even the most handsome man she'd romanced, but his looks pleased her deeply. The smile that had started at the airport was growing by the minute.

'I think this garden is wonderful,' she sighed, gazing around her.

'Yes, it's perfect,' he agreed.

A touch of constraint in his voice made her look at him quickly. 'But you don't like it?'

'I'm—not comfortable with perfection,' he said after a moment. 'For me, it is too precise. A man cannot feel free in a place like this.' He checked himself abruptly and gave a polite smile.

'Where can he feel free?' she asked, her interest growing every moment.

'When he's up high among the birds, where the golden eagles fly so close that it feels as though he's their brother.'

'Golden eagles?' she echoed eagerly. 'Where?'

'In my home in the mountains. I come here very little. My real home is Montedoro.'

'Let me see—monte means a mountain, and "oro" is gold. Is that right?'

'You know Italian?'

'My mother's sister married an Italian. When I was a child we visited them every summer.'

'And you are right. It is "mountain of gold".'

'Because of the golden eagles?'

'Partly. But also because it's the first place the sun touches at dawn, and the last place it leaves at sunset. It's the most beautiful place on earth.'

'It sounds like it,' Angie said wistfully.

He gave her a curious look. 'Would you—?' He broke off with a grunt of embarrassed laughter. 'That is, I wonder if—?'

'Yes?' she encouraged him.

Bernardo drew a deep breath while Angie waited eagerly for what she was sure he was going to say.

'Hey—Bernardo.'

He came back to himself with a start. Angie had the strangest feeling of waking from a dream. And there was Lorenzo, coming along the path, hailing them. 'Time to get ready for dinner,' he called.

As Angie returned to the house with the two of them she was disappointed but not discouraged. Bernardo wanted to show her his home, she was certain of it, and she was every moment growing more eager to learn all about him. The evening lay ahead, and if she couldn't tempt that invitation out of him, she was losing her touch.

She joined Heather in their room and threw herself onto her bed, putting her hands behind her head, with a sigh of pleasure.

'C.H. or S.A?'

'S.A.,' Angie said happily. 'Definitely S.A.'

Heather looked alarmed. 'You be careful!'

'I don't know what you mean,' Angie said innocently.

'Oh, yes, you do. I've seen you when you've set your heart on twisting a man around your little finger. You've got all the tried and tested tricks and a few you invented. But Bernardo doesn't strike me as a man to be fooled with.'

'He isn't,' Angie confirmed. 'He's terribly serious and thoughtful.' She chuckled. 'That's why he's going to be such a challenge.'

'I give up.'

'Yes, do, darling. I'm beyond redemption.'

For dinner she wore a dress of blues and greens in the kind of glowing shades that belonged on a peacock. Many blondes couldn't have got away with it, but Angie looked like a star. She wondered if Bernardo would think so.

She had her answer as she descended the great stairway a little behind Heather, and had the satisfaction of seeing Bernardo look right past the bride, the official guest of honour, to seek out herself. There was even more satisfaction in the subtle change that came over him at the sight of her. He became more alive, every inch of him responding to her as intensely as she was responding to him. She felt a tingle of happy expectancy deep inside as he took her hand and began to take her around his friends and family, introducing her.

Now that she had a chance to study Lorenzo more closely she realised how delightful he was, and she could understand her serious minded friend being bowled over by him. Perhaps he was a touch immature, but his looks and charm were both overwhelming, and no doubt he would soon grow up.

But she couldn't warm to Renato, who struck her as an unpleasant, cynical man, harsh and overbearing. He was tall and splendidly built, but although there was no doubt about his physical attractions, and he greeted her pleasantly, she disliked him, and she could see that her friend was going to have to fight him some time soon.

There were two long tables, each seating thirty. The Martellis were the great family of the area, and the wedding was the event of the year. Baptista headed one table, with the bride and groom. Renato and Bernardo headed the other. Renato was an accomplished host, but Bernardo gave most of his attention to the lady by his side. Perhaps this was fair, as, being English, she needed to have Sicilian cuisine explained to her.

'Bean fritters?' he offered. 'Or perhaps you would prefer stuffed rice ball fritters, or orange salad?'

'That's just one course?' Angie asked, wide-eyed.

'Certainly. The next course is the rice and pasta dishes, pasta with cauliflower, sardines—'

'Yum, yum. Lead me to it.'

Like many petite women Angie could eat like a starved lion without gaining an ounce. This she proceeded to do, to Bernardo's delight. He watched entranced as she demolished a dish of rabbit in sweet and sour sauce, then pressed her to fried pastries with ricotta cheese, which she accepted with relish.

'I have never seen a woman eat like you,' he said admiringly. Then horrified realisation dawned, 'No, I didn't mean it like that! I meant—' He stopped, for Angie was convulsed. Her laughter had a rich, resonant quality that made him smile. He felt his embarrassment evaporate. She understood, and everything was all right. Of course it was.

'I'm an awkward clod,' he said. 'I never know the right thing to say.'

She made a face. 'Who wants to be saying the right thing all the time? It's more interesting if people say what they really mean.'

'Some of the things I say and mean disconcert people,' he admitted ruefully.

'I can imagine.'

The meal was ending, the guests were rising from the table and splitting into groups. Bernardo drew her aside, oblivious to his duties to the other guests. Nor was he the only brother being a poor host. Renato had just returned after twice leaving the table to take a phone call. Bernardo saw her looking in his direction.

'Renato is the Worker of the family and Lorenzo the Charmer,' he said.

'And what are you?'

'I don't know,' he said simply.

He took two glasses from a passing waiter, handed one to her and led the way through a small side door. He hadn't asked if she wanted to draw apart with him, but there had been no need. Angie slipped her hand in his and went gladly.

Away from the dining room the house was quiet. Their feet clicked softly against the floor tiles and the sound echoed in the gloom.

'Where are you taking me?' Angie asked.

He looked surprised. 'Nowhere. I just wanted to be alone with you. Is that all right?'

She smiled, liking his awkward bluntness better than the smooth charm of the men she knew. 'Yes,' she said. 'That's all right.'

He showed her over the vast magnificence of the house, with its great windows that gave onto glorious views no matter which side they faced, its long tapestry hung corridors, and ornate rooms.

'This is the picture gallery,' he said, showing her into a long room, hung with portraits. 'That was Vincente, my father,' he said, indicating a portrait nearest the door. 'The one next to him was his father, then his brother, and so on.'

There were too many faces to take in all at once, but Angie's attention was held by a small picture, almost lost among the others, showing a man dressed in eighteenth-century style, with a sharp, wary face, regarding the world with suspicion.

'Lodovico Martelli,' Bernardo told her. 'About ten generations back.'

'But it's you,' she said in wonder.

'There's a slight resemblance,' he conceded.

'Slight, nothing. It's you to the life. You're a true Martelli.'

'In some ways,' he said after a moment.

She couldn't pursue the subject, because she remembered just in time that what she knew of his situation didn't come from him.

They strolled out onto the terrace. Night had fallen, and in the velvety blackness the only lights came from the house behind them.

He was bound to kiss her now, she thought, and she found she was longing for it to happen. He was different from all other men, and his kisses would be different too. Through the few inches that separated them she could feel him trembling.

Then he did something that left her completely taken aback. Slowly he took her hand in his two hands, raised it, and laid it gently against his cheek.

'Perhaps—' he said, and seemed unable to continue.

'Yes?'

'Perhaps—we should be getting back to the others. I'm being a very bad host.'

With another man she would have said, I think you're being the perfect host, in a teasing voice and a smile that would tell him she was interested. But the flirtatious banter died on her lips. Somehow, with Bernardo, the words wouldn't get themselves said.

'Perhaps you're right,' she said. 'We ought to go back.'

CHAPTER TWO

BERNARDO'S dream was always the same. The young boy was alone in the house, waiting for the return of his mother. The boy was himself, but he could stand aside and watch him, knowing everything he was thinking and feeling as the darkness fell and the knock on the door told him that the world had changed forever. His mother would never return. She lay dead at the bottom of the mountain, trapped with his father in the smashed wreck of a car.

Like a slide show the scene changed. The boy was there again, fighting back the tears over his mother's body, making frantic, grief-stricken promises, to protect her memory, to honour her forever. For her neighbours had called her *prostituta*, and the fact that her lover had been a great man made no real difference, except on the surface. They'd deferred to her, because otherwise Vincente Martelli would have made them suffer. But she was still a *prostituta*.

He'd known, and he'd sworn to erase that stain, to become a strong man like his father and force them to respect her memory. But he'd had to break his promises almost at once.

A different scene. Himself, hiding in the darkness of his mother's house while the argument raged about what to do with him, for he was only twelve, too young to live alone, and the house now belonged to his dead father's family. There'd been talk of an institution. He was a *bastardo*. He had no rights and no name.

Another knock on the door, and the world changed

again. Outside stood a beautiful, frail woman in her forties. Signora Baptista Martelli, his father's betrayed wife, who must surely hate him. But she only smiled sadly and said she had come to take him home.

He'd wept then, to his eternal shame, for he considered himself too old for weeping. But the sobs had devastated him, making it impossible to explain that this was his home and he wanted no other. Having started, he couldn't stop. He wept for days, and all the while everything he loved and valued was taken away from him, and the wealthy Martellis swallowed him up, a helpless prisoner.

It was at this point in the dream that Bernardo always awoke to find his pillow wet and his body shaking. He would be in his room at the Residenza, for the nightmare came to him nowhere else. It stripped away the twenty years that had passed since, making him a grieving, helpless child again, instead of the hard, confident man that the world saw.

He pulled on some jeans and went, bare-chested, out onto the small balcony outside his window. The cool night air awoke him properly and he stood holding onto the rail, feeling the distress fade until he could cope with it again.

Tomorrow he would leave this place and return to his home in the mountains, among his mother's people, where he belonged. He would come back in time for the wedding.

Below he could see the broad terrace. A flicker of white curtain caught his eye and he knew it came from the room where the bride and her companion slept. He wished he hadn't thought of that, for it seemed to bring Angie there before him, teasing as nobody had ever teased him before, bringing warmth to his hard, joyless life.

So strong was the vision that when he heard her soft laughter floating up he didn't at first realise that she was

really there. But then a very real, human voice said, 'Psst!'
and he looked down to see her sitting on the stone ledge
of the terrace, gazing impishly up at him.

He was a man of few social graces. His brothers would
have appreciated the audience, Renato with cynical spec-
ulation, Lorenzo with amused relish. Bernardo tensed, affronted at being looked at when he was unaware, and
horribly conscious of his bare chest. But then he noticed
how the moonlight picked out her slender legs, and the
way her hair was fluffed up as though she'd only just risen
from bed, and he thought—he was almost sure—that beneath her short robe she had nothing on.

A stern sense of propriety made him try to ignore the
thought—after all, she was a guest in the house. But there
was no ignoring the impish way she looked up at him, or
the way his own body was responding to the thought of
her nakedness.

'This is all wrong, you know,' she called.

'What's all wrong?' he asked, suspicious at not understanding her.

'It's Juliet who's supposed to stand on the balcony, and
Romeo who looks up from below.'

Her voice carried sweetly on the night air, like the singing of nightingales, and he could only look at her dumbly.

'Aren't you going to say anything?' she asked, her head
on one side, like a pretty, expectant little bird.

'Yes—I was going to ask if you rose to see the dawn.
It will be very soon.'

'I expect it's lovely.'

'It's lovely here, but even more so in my home, because
it is so high.' He took a deep breath and forced himself
to say, 'I'm glad to see you now, because I have to leave
very early tomorrow, to return there.'

'Oh.' That was all she said, but the disappointed droop

in her voice was more than he could bear. The next words came out despite his determination that they shouldn't. 'Perhaps you would care to come with me.'

'I'd love to.'

'We leave very early.'

'*No way!*' she almost squeaked, trying to remember the sleepers in the house and express her outrage at the same time. 'I get up early when I go to work. I'm on holiday.' She almost danced with indignation.

He grinned, enchanted by her. 'I'll wait for you. Now be off back to bed, or you'll oversleep.'

She laughed and vanished. Bernardo stayed a long time looking at the place where she'd been. He knew he'd done something dangerous to his peace. If he was wise he would write her an apologetic note, leave it with a servant, and depart at once.

But he wasn't going to. Because suddenly he didn't want to be wise.

Next morning was a bustle of departure. Lorenzo was off to Stockholm to finish some work before the wedding. Renato was taking Heather sailing so that she could decide whether to accept the offer of his yacht for the honeymoon. Angie politely declined the offer to accompany them, explaining that she was going to the mountains with Bernardo.

'You be careful,' Heather warned.

Angie smiled, thinking of last night, and the way the silver moonlight had limned Bernardo's chest and the muscles of his shoulders and arms. 'Where's the fun in being careful?' she murmured to herself, as she got into the shower.

She chose her clothes thoughtfully. White jeans, with a deep blue silk top that turned her eyes to violet. It was slightly stretchy, and clung in a way that showed what a nice shape she had. Dainty silver sandals and a silver filigree necklace and matching earrings completed her appearance, and a discreet squirt of a very expensive perfume provided the finishing touch.

She was prompt, but even so he was waiting for her beside his car, a four-wheel drive, made for rough terrain. It was like the man, nothing fancy, but powerful, uncompromising, made to last.

He swung out of Palermo and into the countryside. After a while they began to climb, and before long they'd reached a small village with narrow, twisting streets. At the top of a hill stood a pretty pink villa with two curved staircases on the outside.

'This village is Ellona,' Bernardo told her. 'It mostly belongs to Baptista. So does the villa. We used to live there in the summer. In fact, that was where—' He braked suddenly as a chicken darted across the road and uttered something in Sicilian that sounded like a curse.

'What did that mean?' Angie asked.

He coloured. 'Never mind. I shouldn't have said it.'

'Go on with what you were saying. That was where—?'

'I forget. Look at the scenery just up here. It's magnificent.'

It wasn't just her imagination, she thought. After the first slip of the tongue he'd retreated back in on himself and, when she tried to follow, he'd warned her off. She wasn't foolish enough to persist.

Away from the fertile coast the landscape of Sicily changed, become harsher, more barren.

'All the prosperity is on the coast,' Bernardo said. 'Inland we live as we can. There are crops, sheep, goats. Sometimes we do well, but it's a precarious existence.'

'We?' she asked.

'My people,' he said simply. 'The ones who depend on me.'

After a while he asked, 'Does the height worry you? Some people get scared as the road twists and turns.'

'Not me,' she said bravely, although her eyes were getting a little glazed. 'How high are we now?'

'Nearly half a mile above sea level.'

Higher and higher they went on the winding mountain road, while the glory of Sicily fell away beneath them. Everywhere Angie looked there were acacia and lemon blossom, and far distant she could make out the gleam of the sea.

The scenery grew fiercer, grander. They were passing through pinewoods, then the woods were behind them and an upland plain spread out, with vineyards and, above them, a steep cliff with farmhouses.

'The farmers abandoned them long ago,' Bernardo said. 'This is a harsh place to live in winter.'

After a few more miles he pointed and said, 'Look.'

She rose in her seat, gasping in amazement and delight at the sight that met her eyes. Ahead of them was a village that seemed to have been carved direct from the very rock that reared up to a windswept promontory. What might have been a bleak and uncompromising scene was softened to beauty by the reddish colour of the sheer rock face. She sat back, gazing in wonder as they drove closer, and she saw that this was actually an enchanting little medieval town, whose delights had to be seen up close to be appreciated.

'That's Montedoro,' Bernardo said. 'Most of it is seven hundred years old.'

They drove in through an ancient gateway and immediately began to climb a steep, beautifully cobbled street, the Corso Garibaldi, according to the signs. It was lined with shops, many of which seemed to sell sweets and pastries. Faces watched them curiously, and it was clear that everyone knew who Bernardo was. She wondered about the size of the village. From the outside it hadn't seemed very big.

He drove very slowly, for the streets were crowded with tourists. At one point a cart turned out of a street directly in front of them, forcing them to slow to a walk. It contained five people and was drawn by two mules sporting tassels and feathers. But what really drew Angie's attention was the fact that the cart was brightly decorated in every possible place.

'Is that one of the Sicilian hand-painted carts I've heard about?' she asked eagerly.

'That's right. My friend Benito and his son make a summer living giving rides in their carts.'

Travelling so slowly, she had time to study the glorious paintwork. The wheels, including the spokes were covered in patterns, while on the main body were pictures of saints, warriors and dragons, all glowing in the brilliant sun.

At the top of the street he swung right along a pretty street of grey stone houses, all with ironwork balconies, and at the end of that he swung right again, heading downwards to a building that Angie gradually recognised as the gate where they'd entered.

'But—that's—'

'Montedoro is a perfect triangle,' he said with a grin. 'Now we'll go up the Corso Garibaldi again, to my house.'

When they reached the top she saw a small piazza with several boutiques, and a café with tables spilling onto the street, each one sheltered by a brightly coloured awning.

He parked the car and headed for one of the shops, so it seemed to Angie, but at the last minute he swerved aside, to a lane so narrow that she hadn't seen it. It went right to the back of the shop where it crossed with another lane. Here the space was so cramped and the houses so tall that it was almost dark. When Angie's eyes were used to the gloom she saw a narrow door in the wall.

'Welcome to my home,' Bernardo said, throwing open the door to a world of magic.

She entered with wonder. Instead of the dark hallway she'd expected, she found herself in a courtyard, open to the sky. Delicately arched cloisters went around the sides, and in the centre was a fountain whose water caught the brilliant sun on every droplet.

'I never expected—I mean, I never thought you'd live in a place like this,' she breathed.

'My father bought it for my mother. Lots of the houses in Montedoro have these little courtyards, so that women and children could sit here, and not have to go into the outside world.'

'A man who believed in the traditional ways,' Angie observed.

'Yes, and also because people were often unkind to my mother because they weren't married. So he protected her.'

'It's incredible, how it's hidden away,' she marvelled. 'From outside those shops you'd never guess that it was here, unless you knew where that passage was, and even then you might miss it.'

'That's the idea. Outside the world bustles, especially in summer, when this place is a tourist trap. Then all the shops open for the foreign visitors, and the great families from Palermo come up here to open their summer houses and escape the heat. But then summer passes, the visitors go, and only the basic population is left.'

'How many would that be?'

'About six hundred. It's like a ghost town.'

'How do the people live when there are no visitors?'

'Many of them work in the vineyards you saw below. The Martelli family owns them and I run them.'

Again she noticed the slight oddity in his speech, the way he spoke of 'the Martelli family' as though he wasn't one of them.

Deep in the house she heard the telephone ring. He excused himself and went to answer it. Left alone, Angie looked around the little courtyard. It wasn't expensively tended and perfect like the garden at the Residenza, but it had an austere elegance that pleased her.

She sat on the side of the stone fountain and looked into the water. Above her the impossibly blue sky was reflected clearly, and just behind her she saw Bernardo appear. He was looking at her, and she wondered if he'd forgotten that she could see his face in the water, because he wore an expression that made her catch her breath. It was the look of a man who'd been taken by surprise and held against his will. There was alarm, yearning, and a touch of wistfulness. Then he stepped back quickly and his face vanished. When Angie glanced up he wasn't looking at her.

A large woman of about fifty emerged from the kitchen. Bernardo introduced her as Stella, his house keeper. Stella greeted Angie in excellent English, informing them that wine and snacks were waiting for them, while she finished cooking the proper meal. The snacks turned out to be bean fritters, hot cheese and herbs, and stuffed baked tomatoes.

'If this is only a snack, I can't wait to see what the full meal is like,' Angie mused.

'It will be a feast,' he said, pouring her a glass of Marsala. 'Stella is delighted to see you. She loves displaying her cooking, and I so seldom bring guests here.'

Glass in hand, he began showing her his home. Despite its beauty it was an austere place, with the bare minimum of dark, heavy oak furniture. The floors were covered with smooth flagstones with the occasional rag rug. The walls were plain stone or brick. There were some pictures, but they weren't the valuable old masters of the Residenza. One was a photograph, an aerial view of Montedoro itself, touched by the sun and standing proud against the valley far below. One was a childish watercolour, showing the streets of the little town, and a man in the dark clothes Bernardo himself was wearing.

'Yes, that's meant to be me,' he said, smiling as he saw her gaze. 'It was done by the children of the local convent school after I paid for them to go have a day out.'

Looking more closely, Angie saw the word *Grazie* along the bottom of the picture. 'It's charming,' she said. 'Do you often give them treats?'

He shrugged. 'A party at Christmas, a trip to the theatre. It's a tiny school. It costs me next to nothing.'

Stella appeared from the kitchen, anxious to speak to him, and while he turned away Angie continued looking around. One door stood ajar, and through the three-inch crack she could just see the end of a bed. After struggling with her better self for a moment she ventured to push it a little further open.

The room was dominated by a large brass bedstead. The walls were stone, the floor made of red flagstones, with one rug beside the bed. There was one cane chair and one pine table on which Bernardo kept his few possessions. It might have been a monk's cell, except for the old-fashioned picture of a woman by the bed. Angie had seen the portrait of Bernardo's ancestor, but now she saw his mother, and realised how both of them were subtly blended in him.

It was an intriguing face. The woman had been beautiful with a heavy sensual mouth that hovered on the edge of a smile. But there was something about the eyes, an ironic watchfulness, a refusal to compromise, that spoilt her for Angie. But she was being unfair, she reflected. This woman had been trapped in a situation that left her much to endure. She had coped, but Angie, a woman from a totally different culture, guessed it had twisted her nature out of true, and some of her tensions had been passed on to her son.

The mystery about Bernardo deepened.

She was too cautious to linger, and slipped out quickly before he returned.

In one room the medieval atmosphere had been banished by a modern computer, a desk and filing cabinets.

'This is where I do my paperwork,' he said with a grimace. 'Thank goodness for technology, so that I can do as little as possible.'

On the far side were huge windows reflecting the blue of the sky, both slightly ajar. Angie strode over and threw them open to take a deep breath, and found herself looking straight down the long drop into the valley. She gasped and turned away, her head spinning.

In a flash Bernardo was beside her, his arms about her waist, holding her steady. 'I should have warned you that that window opens straight onto the drop,' he said.

'I'm all right. I haven't much head for heights—it just took me by surprise. Phew!'

'Come away from the window,' he said, drawing her into the room. 'That's better.'

His clasp about her waist was light, but even so, she

could sense the steely power of the man, and it thrilled
her. Her heart was beating in anticipation. They were so
close that she could feel the heat of his body and inhale
his spicy, male aroma. And surely he must sense her own
reaction to him. Even a man so lacking in polish must
know that he delighted her. Some things could be neither
faked nor hidden.

The next moment she met his eyes and saw in them
everything she wanted. But he released her nonetheless,
setting a careful distance between them and saying in a
voice that wasn't quite steady,

'Stella will have lunch ready by now. We mustn't keep
her excellent food waiting.'

The table was laid in a simple room next to the kitchen
with red flagstones, white walls, and a pair of French windows that opened onto the cloisters. Through these a gentle breeze blew, and they had a view straight out onto the
fountain.

'It's magic,' she breathed, as they sat down to eat.

'It is at this time of year. In winter, very few people
would find it magic. At this height the cold can be dread-
ful. Sometimes I look out of my window and all I can see
is snow and mist, cutting the valley off. It's like floating
above the clouds.'

'But then you can go down and live at the Residenza?'

'I could. But I don't.'

'But isn't it equally your home?'

'No,' he said briefly. He glanced up and said, 'I'm sure
you've heard the story.'

'Some of it,' she admitted. 'How could I help knowing
when you're so prickly about it?'

'Am I?'

'At the airport, Lorenzo introduced you as his brother,

and you hurried to say, "Half-brother". It was like you wanted everyone to know you were different.'

'Not really. I just don't like to sail under false colours.'

'But isn't that the same thing in different words?' she asked gently.

After a moment he said, 'Yes, I suppose it is.'

'Why won't you let yourself be one of the family?'

'Because I'm not,' he said simply. 'I never can be. I was born a part of another family, my mother and my father. My name was Bernardo Tornese. To the people here it still is.'

'Only to them?'

He hesitated. 'Legally I am Martelli. Baptista changed my name when I was still a child, unable to prevent it.'

'But she must have meant to be kind, giving you your father's name.'

'I know, and I honour her for it, as I honour her for all her kindness. It can't have been easy for her to take me in and live with the constant reminder of her husband's infidelity.

'She's been good to me in other ways, too. My father bought this house and several other properties in the village, presumably meaning them to pass to my mother, and then to me. But when he died they were still in his name, and they became Baptista's. She said they were mine by right, signed them over to me, and administered them until I was of age.'

'What a magnificent woman!'

'Yes. Her sense of duty towards me has never failed.'

'But was it only duty? Perhaps she was fond of you as well?'

He frown. 'How could she be? Think how she must have hated my mother!'

'Has she ever behaved as though she did?'

'Never. She has treated me like her own sons, but I've always wondered what lay beneath it.'

Angie was about to say something conventionally polite about Baptista's motives when she remembered her impression of yesterday, that beneath the charming surface the old woman had a steely will.

'How did you come to meet her?' she asked.

'She turned up here a few days after my parents' death, and said she'd come to take me to my father's home. I didn't want to go, but I had no choice. As soon as I could, I ran away.'

'And came back here,' Angie said at once, and was rewarded by his smile at her understanding.

'Yes, I came back here, where I felt I belonged. Of course I was fetched back, but I escaped again. This time I hid out in the mountains, and when they found me I had a fever. By the time I was well again, I knew it was useless to run away. Many women, in Baptista's position would have left me to my fate, and I suppose I was an ungrateful wretch—'

'But you were a child and you'd just lost your parents,' Angie said sympathetically. 'No wonder you weren't thinking straight.'

'Yes. If it had happened a little later, I think I could have appreciated her generosity more. As it was, I saw only an attempt to wipe my mother out of the record. That's why I cling to her name. Inside myself I am still Bernardo Tornese.'

Since he'd opened up so far Angie ventured to ask, 'What were you going to tell me about Ellona, as we drove up?'

'The villa you saw there is part of the estate of Bella Rosaria which belongs to Baptista. That was where she took me after I recovered from the fever. I used to awaken in the night and hear her weeping for my father's death.'

His face was troubled and Angie held her breath, feeling something happen here that was beautiful and mysterious. But before she could speak he forced a smile and said, 'Why are we talking about sad things? Let us take our wine outside.'

The shadows were beginning to lengthen and it was deliciously cool by the fountain. Smiling, she watched their reflections. But then something made her look up, and what she saw in Bernardo's eyes caused the breath to catch in her throat.

Slowly he took her hand in his and held it for a moment, touching it almost reverently. He said nothing, and in the silence Angie could hear her heart hammering. He wasn't even kissing her, just holding her hand as hesitantly as a boy, yet she could feel herself responding so intensely that she was almost scared.

It wasn't supposed to be like this. Always before she'd been in control. Suddenly she wasn't in control of anything, especially her own feelings. She felt like someone who'd set out to take a pleasant day trip and found themselves clinging onto a runaway train. In another moment he really would kiss her, and she wanted it more than she'd ever wanted anything in her life.

The soft shrill of his mobile phone shattered the moment. Bernardo took a long breath and answered it reluctantly. 'Yes?' he said, sounding ragged.

Angie watched a change come over his face as he listened. Finally he said, 'We'll be right there.' He shut off the phone and said, 'That was Renato. There's been an accident on the boat. Heather nearly drowned. He asks that you go to her at once.'

'Of course.'

On the way down the mountain he explained tersely, 'She and Renato went out on the Jet Ski, and she fell off. When he turned back to look for her she'd gone under. It sounds like a nasty moment. Luckily he found her fairly quickly. He called me from the boat. They should reach the port about the same time we do.'

At last the port of Mondello came into view. The *Santa Maria* was just tying up. Angie jumped from the car while it was still moving and took Renato's outstretched hand onto the boat.

She found Heather sleeping in the big bedroom. To Angie's relief her colour was good and she was breathing normally. She woke at Angie's touch and gave her a sleepy smile.

'Trust you to get in the wars,' Angie said. 'Renato sent for me.'

Heather eyed her wickedly, 'I hope you weren't interrupted at too difficult a moment.'

'There'll be others,' Angie said, conscious that she was colouring. 'I want you to spend tomorrow in bed. We'll leave as soon as you're better.'

Renato drove them home, Angie travelling in the same car as Heather, and Bernardo following on behind. She tried to give her friend all her attention, but inwardly she was thinking of Montedoro, another world, where eagles soared and spirits were free.

CHAPTER THREE

BERNARDO remained at the Residenza next day, but they had little time alone. Angie felt duty-bound to stay close to Heather, who slept most of the time under the influence of a sedative. Also, she found herself caught up in a family crisis.

'Renato called Lorenzo,' Bernardo told her. 'But he'd checked out of his hotel in Stockholm this morning.'

'But—I don't understand. He was supposed to stay until tomorrow.'

'I know. But he's gone, and nobody knows where.'

'He's not playing fast and loose, is he?' Angie demanded suspiciously.

'How do you mean?'

'Having a final fling before the wedding. I've heard about continental men.'

'I'll be—!' Bernardo exclaimed, nettled. 'That's not only unjust, it's bigoted, prejudiced—and I don't know what. It's practically racist. In fact, it *is* racist.'

'Well, Italians do have rather a reputation.' Angie said illogically.

'Does that mean Lorenzo lives up to it? Do all Englishmen act the same way?'

'Well, no. But I don't know Lorenzo well enough to say what he is like. And, as his brother, you probably do.'

He sighed and ran his hands through his hair. 'Yes, I'm sorry.'

'No, I'm sorry. It's not your fault.'

He looked at her with a little smile that made her heart turn over. 'I think we just had our first quarrel.'

'So we did.'

They exchanged rueful glances and he opened his arms, pulling her into a hug.

Our first quarrel, she thought. *Before our first kiss. And if I didn't want that kiss so badly I wouldn't be on edge now.*

With the house in a bustle there was no chance of developing the hug into something interesting. Footsteps in the corridor made them pull apart hastily. The next moment Renato entered, looking exasperated.

'The mystery is solved,' he said. 'Lorenzo has just called to say he's on his way home. Apparently he decided this morning to skip all his appointments and come back.' His voice grated with displeasure on the last words.

'He couldn't bear to stay away from Heather,' Angie sighed. 'That's sweet.'

'It's not sweet,' Renato snapped. 'He had work to do, work he was already behind with.'

'He's getting married in a few days—' Angie protested.

'Is he at the airport now?' Bernardo put in quickly before an argument could start.

'No, he was calling from Rome, where he had to make a connection. He'll be here in about three hours.'

'Fine,' Angie said crisply. 'I'll tell Heather.'

She favoured him with a glare before walking out smartly, closely followed by Bernardo.

'I pity Heather,' she said crossly. 'I really do. Fancy having Renato as a brother-in-law.'

'Perhaps she loves Lorenzo enough not to mind being related to Renato,' Bernardo observed. 'They say love can do that to people.'

It flashed across her mind that he might not be talking

about Heather and Lorenzo. For he himself was related to Renato, and if—

Don't be absurd! This is a holiday romance. He hasn't even kissed you yet!

Lorenzo's return changed things, but not in the way she'd expected. He arrived that afternoon, looking harassed, and it didn't seem to Angie that this was a man who'd tossed everything aside to be with his beloved. Instead he hurried to find Renato and the two of them spent the rest of the day closeted in the study, from behind whose door Angie could hear agitated voices.

Perhaps Lorenzo was berating his brother for not taking better care of Heather. She certainly hoped so. She wondered when she would have another chance to be alone with Bernardo.

It came the next day. Lorenzo, looking pale and tense, was swept off by Renato to work at the company's head office in Palermo, while Baptista claimed Heather's company.

'Naturally, we'd be glad if you joined us,' she said with a smile, 'but I expect you and Bernardo have made other plans.'

'Well—'

'Of course you have. And when the wedding is over I hope you won't feel you have to hurry back to England. Perhaps you could stay another week?'

'Thank you, I'd like that,' Angie said, feeling the sun come out inside her.

This time it was her choice to go to Montedoro. Bernardo offered to show her the island, but she wanted to return to his eagle kingdom, where he was most completely himself.

When they were part of the way up the mountain he turned the car onto the grass and they got out and walked under the trees. From here Sicily was spread out before them in all its glory. Above them birds sang, the trees were in full beauty and the sky was an unbelievable blue. Angie stopped to breathe in the sweet air. The next moment she felt his hand tighten on hers, and she was in his arms.

The feel of his lips locked onto hers sent happiness streaming through her. She kissed him back, fervently, eagerly, inviting him to kiss her more deeply. She felt his clasp grow more confident. He'd understand her at once, and they could bypass the first tentative questions that strangers needed to ask, for they had never been strangers. They'd known each other from the first moment in the airport, and this sweet blazing kiss had been inevitable then.

His lips were just as she had known they would be, firm and decisive, and her own responded frankly, no holding back. To have pretended reserve would have been a kind of dishonesty, when in truth her heart was reaching out to him.

Just now they asked little of each other, an eager embrace and lips seeking lips, exchanging warmth. She caught a glimpse of his face and he was almost smiling, like a man who'd discovered longed-for treasure and found it all he'd dreamed. There was a hint of surprise as well and it touched her heart. It was as though joy was so unfamiliar to him that he hardly dared to claim it as his own.

He trailed the fingers of one hand slowly down her cheek, almost as though he couldn't believe she was really there. His words confirmed it.

'You won't vanish, will you? I've thought of this since the moment we met, and now—'

'I'm not going anywhere,' she said happily.

'Except with me?'

'Except with you.'

'Kiss me—kiss me—' His lips were on hers again before she had the chance to speak. Suddenly she was aware of everything in the world about her. The sun had never been so warm, the air so sweet, life so worth living.

Bernardo drew back a little. He was shaking. 'We must go on to Montedoro,' he said unsteadily. 'I don't trust myself to be alone with you.' He kissed her briefly one more time. 'Let's go.'

Reluctantly she placed her hand in his and followed him to the car. She was moving in a happy dream, and it lasted all the way up the mountain.

Montedoro was in its full summer prosperity, bursting with tourists. To make the chaos worse, it was market day, and fifty stalls were crammed into the tiny piazza at the highest point of the little town. Every stall keeper greeted him with a cry of, *'E, Signor Bernardo,'* and inclined their head courteously to Angie. Sometimes he merely waved and passed on. Sometimes he stopped to talk, always introducing her, and she became aware that she was being watched curiously on all sides.

They stopped for tea at a tiny convent where the Superior, Mother Francesca, welcomed him as a benefactor and a small, elderly nun made him swear not to leave until he'd tried her new batch of cakes. He solemnly promised, and Angie found herself eating the most delicious almond cakes she'd ever tasted.

Again she could feel the curious eyes on all sides and a frisson went up her spine. It was almost as though Bernardo was showing her to 'his people' for a purpose. But that was nonsense. This was a brief flirtation. Nothing more.

But her inner questions were like wisps of smoke. What was happening was out of her control.

While she was just trying to decide on another cake she heard someone knocking on the front door. The sound was faint, muffled by the thick stone walls, but she could just make out that the door was opened, for the knocking ceased, to be replaced by shouting, and the sound of a child crying. Then there were footsteps in the corridor. Mother Francesca hurried out and returned a moment later, looking troubled.

'A little girl has been knocked down in the street and Dr Fortuno is away,' she said. 'So they've brought her to Sister Ignatia, our infirmary nurse.'

Bernardo glanced quickly at Angie who immediately said, 'I'm a doctor. Can I help?'

'I'd be so grateful,' the nun replied. 'We're worried in case the child has some broken bones.'

The convent infirmary was a small room, with a bed, equipped for little more than first aid. On the bed was lying a little girl of about eight, crying bitterly. With her was an old woman dressed in black. She had a lined, nut brown face and white hair, covered by a black headscarf. Sister Ignatia spoke to her in Sicilian, indicating Angie, and immediately the old woman was up in arms, standing between them and letting forth a stream of Sicilian whose meaning was only too clear.

Sister Ignatia silenced her, explaining that Angie was a doctor, which at first the woman flatly refused to believe. This was a young woman. How could she be a doctor? Even without knowing the words Angie was able to follow this without trouble.

But it seemed there was another problem. The old woman refused to be placated, pointing at Angie's trousers with an expression of outrage.

'I'm sorry,' Bernardo said, embarrassed. 'This is a very old fashioned place, and especially the older generation—'

'You mean my trousers bother her?' Angie asked.

'At one time—the only women who wore them—' Bernardo broke off in embarrassment.

'Were "bad" women,' Angie finished for him. 'It's all right. I understand.'

Bernardo tried to speak to the grandmother. Her attitude immediately became deferential and it was clear to Angie that he was the local 'great man'. But there was a point beyond which deference did not go, even for him, and she remained obdurate.

'It's no use,' Angie told him. 'You're the wrong person.' She turned to the Reverend Mother. 'If *you* vouch for my good character, surely this lady will accept your word?'

The Superior nodded and immediately broke into rapid speech. The old woman's face began to relax and she glanced at Angie uncertainly. But still she didn't yield, until the little girl gave a loud cry and sobbed more bitterly than ever.

'That's it, I'm going to work,' Angie said firmly. She stepped forward, and to her relief the grandmother didn't try to hinder her.

She began examining the patient who, to her relief, wasn't seriously injured. There were some nasty cuts and bruises but nothing was broken. With Sister Ignatia's help she cleaned the child up, and bathed and dressed her cuts.

Then, mindful of professional etiquette, she said, 'You should let Dr Fortuno see her when he returns. He may want to send her for X-rays, but I don't think so. If he wants to talk to me I'll be glad to discuss what I've done.'

She finished with a smile at the little girl, who smiled

back, evidently having decided that this was a good person. The grandmother watched them both closely. So did the nuns. So did Bernardo.

When they left he became quiet, walking with his fingers entwined with hers but saying nothing. Sometimes he would look at her with a curious little smile.

'What is it?' she asked.

'You look different all the time. There are so many of you.'

'No, there's only one of me. Truly.'

'Then you have a thousand faces. I no longer seem to know what to say to you.'

'What do you want to say?'

He raised her hand and brushed his lips over it.

'Now I really believe you're a doctor,' he said as they strolled on. 'The way you took charge, dealt with that awkward woman—you were right, of course. She wouldn't have taken a man's word for your good character—even mine—because she thought—well—' he shrugged self-consciously '—but she had to take the Reverend Mother's word for it.'

Noting the unconscious arrogance of that 'even mine', Angie thought that he was more of a Martelli than he wanted to admit, but she only said, 'I can't believe that she got so worked up just because of how I was dressed.'

'It's only twelve years since a Sicilian woman published an autobiographical novel about a girl who became the town outcast because she wanted to wear trousers,' Bernardo told her. 'It was a best-seller in these parts.

'And my mother used to tell me of a woman she'd known who had no chance of marriage because she'd "had a man". Eventually I found out what "had a man" meant. She'd been seen drinking coffee with him at an outside table of a café.'

'And that was all it took?' Angie demanded, aghast.

'That was all it took. It isn't an easy society for a woman, especially one from a strange culture—'

'Did she come from a strange culture?'

'Who?' he asked, sounding startled.

'This woman who had coffee with a man.'

'I don't know where she came from,' he said hurriedly. 'Stella will be waiting for us with a meal.'

Stella had laid herself out to please, with flowers on the table and food served on the best china. The Montedoro grapevine had ensured that she already knew of the day's dramatic events, and she treated Angie with a new touch of deference, anxiously awaiting her verdict on every dish.

'Thank goodness,' Bernardo said when Stella had finally left them to their coffee. 'I've wanted to be alone with you all day, but there was always somebody else, and now the day has gone.'

'Not all of it,' she said. She was standing by a window that looked out over the valley. The darkness was descending, gradually concealing everything except some lights that flickered far below. This was a magic place, she thought happily, and the most perfect magic was to be with Bernardo.

He came to join her. 'I'm glad you've seen my home like this,' he said. 'This is when it's at its most beautiful.'

'I know. I've never seen anything so enchanting.'

'Angie—' He moved his lips towards hers, and she waited, her heart beating.

The scream of the doorbell broke the spell.

'Damn!' Bernardo said violently, jerking backwards. 'Who can it be now?'

It was Dr Fortuno, eager to talk to Angie. He was full of gratitude for her help, overflowing with explanations for his absence—his practice was spread so wide—he couldn't be in two places at once, etc. etc.

He was an elderly man who looked tired from a long day, and even more tired from a long life and a demanding job. Angie swiftly formed the impression that he was a decent, well-meaning doctor in a basic way, but the advances of medical science had left him far behind.

Bernardo concealed his impatience, treated him courteously, plied him with coffee, wine, cakes, and listened with Angie while the old man said everything three times. By the time Dr Fortuno made his way out of the front door, still talking, two hours had passed.

With the door safely closed, Bernardo muttered, *'Malediri!'*

'Is that a Sicilian curse?' Angie asked with a rueful little smile.

'Yes,' he said. 'It certainly is. And now it's time for me to drive you home.' He looked at her.

'Yes, I suppose you should,' Angie agreed doubtfully. 'It's late—they'll be wondering—'

'Yes.'

'If he hadn't called—' she said slowly.

Their eyes met, and they both knew he wasn't going to let her go without kissing her.

'Bernardo...' she whispered, and the next moment she was in his arms, her lips on his, in the kiss she'd dreamed of every moment since their first one that afternoon.

His lips were as warmly possessive as she'd known they would be, and as thrilling. The kiss was like the man himself, ardent, blunt, sincere. All the pent-up frustration of the evening was there in her, and she could feel the same in him. It was like meeting him all over again, but more sweetly, more intensely, and for ever.

'Angie,' he murmured, *'amor mia...'*

'Yes,' she said, feverishly caressing his lips with her own. 'Oh, yes…'

She heard the click as his bedroom door opened, and she moved easily with him until they were inside. The rush of passion that possessed her was driving thought away, turning her into a single flame of desire. They had been made for each other, they'd both known that from the first, and it seemed only a short step to this moment when he drew her down on the bed.

His arms tightened, drawing her fiercely against him. Her lips parted readily to the insistence of his probing tongue and the next moment she felt him, the tip of his tongue flickering provocatively against the sensitive inside of her mouth. Through those movements she was vibrantly aware of every part of him and of herself.

Her whole body was his. It had already belonged to him even before he'd tried to claim it. Excitement was gathering strength within her, propelling her forward to the beauty that awaited, that she was eager for. As his mouth made a burning trail down her neck she arched against him, inviting his deeper exploration, thrilling to the feel of his hands beginning to rove more intimately over her.

And then, at the most beautiful moment, coming out of nowhere, shaking her with alarm, came the thought, *This is more than I want.*

One part of her ached with longing to lie with him and give herself up to her feelings, both physical and emotional. She wanted him, yearned for him. But afterwards? Did she want that? If she made love with this serious man it would no longer be a light-hearted holiday romance, for there was nothing light-hearted about Bernardo. Whatever he did he would do with passionate intensity, meaning everything with his whole soul. But that was too much.

Reluctantly she put up a hand, fending him off. 'Bernardo, no—please—'

She had a glimpse of the fierce light in his eyes, then he shuddered and released her. He turned away fast and held onto the brass end of the bed, breathing hard. When he looked around his eyes were calmer, but his expression was still distraught.

'You're right,' he said in a shaking voice. 'It mustn't be like this. I can't treat you like a—you are more to me than that, more than anything. Forgive me.' He pulled himself together. 'It's late. I must get you home.'

Neither of them spoke as he drove carefully down the mountain, and Angie was glad of the silence. It gave her shattered nerves a chance to calm down, and it also gave her time to ponder the meaning of Bernardo's words. He'd backed off, just as she had, but for the opposite reason. By refusing to make love with her he'd mysteriously taken their relationship into the realms of love and commitment, where she had feared to tread. And with every part of her she found she was glad.

He came with her as far as the downstairs hall, and kissed her cheek as chastely as a boy with his first love. 'Good night,' he said, turning to go.

'Aren't you sleeping here tonight?'

He smiled ruefully. 'I dare not. I can't trust myself to sleep under the same roof with you. When this wedding is over, we—'

'Yes,' she said wistfully. 'We will.'

'Until then—goodnight, my love.'

The last day before the wedding. A shopping trip with Heather and Baptista, who insisted on buying them both gifts. She had seen a dress she thought would suit Heather, and wanted her to have it before the honeymoon.

'I know you'll be sailing most of the time,' she said, 'but when you put into port and go dancing, you will look beautiful in this. My Lorenzo is so lucky.'

While Heather was in the fitting room Baptista gave Angie a conspiratorial smile. 'I'm so grateful to you,' she said. 'These last few days Bernardo has looked happier than at any time since I've known him. Perhaps we'll soon have another wedding.'

'Oh—well—'

'Forgive me,' Baptista said quickly. 'That was clumsy. I would never try to rush you into marriage with Bernardo. He's a strange man, in many ways, not like the other men, but I'm sure you've realised that for yourself.'

'Very much so.' Angie hesitated, 'I know how he comes to be living as your son—'

'To me, he *is* my son. I would gladly love him as I do the other two, for Vincente's sake. It is Bernardo himself who will not allow it. Sadly, he can never regard me as any kind of mother. I think he feels it would be a betrayal of his real mother. There is a Sicilian saying "A man's mother is his soul. If he loses her, he will never find her again."

'Sicily is still a very male-dominated society, almost nineteenth-century in many ways. So it may surprise you to know that our men take this saying seriously. Bernardo takes it very seriously indeed. I think—and I'm guessing, because he doesn't confide in me—that he feels he betrayed his mother's memory by coming to us after her death.

'This may be why he's never allowed himself to be part of the family, although we would have welcomed him. I gave him his father's name, but—' she smiled sadly 'I know he never uses it. He could have had a third of his father's fortune. Lorenzo and Renato agreed that this was just.

'But Bernardo refused. He accepted the property in Montedoro, because my husband had clearly intended it for him. But the rest, the vineyards, the orchards, the canning factories—none of this will he touch, not even the vineyards near Montedoro itself. He administers them, but only for a salary. He has wealthy brothers, but he insists on remaining a relatively poor man, for I don't think the rents on the property up there bring in very much.'

'But why?' Angie asked, frowning. 'I understand about his loyalty to his mother, but that's hardly—I mean—'

'It can only be part of the explanation,' Baptista agreed. 'There must be something else, but we're not close enough for me to ask. Inside him, there's something dark and dangerous, something that holds him back from too much human contact. He can be a generous man, but also a hard and unforgiving one. To the woman he loved he would show a face that nobody else would be allowed to see, but even for her he wouldn't be easy to love. I know only that he is driven by furies, and—and one fury in particular.'

'And that is?'

Baptista sighed. 'It's not my place to speak. I can only guess at his deepest secret, and I may be wrong. When he trusts you with it, you will know he truly loves you.'

Heather emerged from the fitting room in the dress which was as gorgeous on her as Baptista had predicted. In the bustle of preparing to leave, and receiving the diamond brooch Baptista insisted on giving to Angie, the subject was allowed to drop.

That night Heather awoke in the early hours and saw Angie sitting by the window.

'What is it?' she asked anxiously. 'Is something wrong?'

'No, there's nothing wrong,' Angie assured her. 'I'm just enjoying a little laugh against myself.'

Heather got out of bed, pulled on a robe and came to sit beside her. 'It's Bernardo, isn't it?'

'Yes,' Angie said softly. 'It's Bernardo.'

Heather gave her a hug. 'Why were you laughing at yourself?'

'Because I thought I had love taped. I was the one who danced into romance and danced out again when it suited me. It was a game: flirtations, all played with men who were playing the same game, and no hearts broken on either side. Or at least,' she added with rueful honesty, 'not on my side, at any rate.

'I thought Bernardo was going to be just another holiday love. I sized him up, decided he'd be a pleasant pastime for a few days, and took him on. Oh, boy, did I make a mistake!' She gave a shaky laugh. 'I'm not going to dance out of this one.'

'Do you want to?'

'No,' Angie said, half laughing, half tearful. 'I love him so much it hurts. I think about him all the time. He fills my heart.'

'But you've only known him a few days.'

'I know. That's what makes it silliest of all. Just a few days was enough—or a few minutes. I think I knew as soon as we met in the airport. He was the one. He was the reason none of the others ever became too serious. They weren't *him*. I was waiting for him all the time, and now I've found him, I couldn't face life without him.'

'But surely you won't have to. I think he's just as overwhelmed as you. Hasn't he told you?'

'He doesn't use many words,' Angie said, but her eyes told the rest.

'I'm really happy for you. Are you happy?'

'Oh, yes, yes, so happy. If only he'd say something to make it definite!' Angie laughed wildly and buried her face in her hands. 'Isn't it a big joke? I kept them all dangling and it was only fun. But now someone's keeping me dangling and it isn't fun any more. Angie's met her match.' She raised her head. Her mouth was curved in a blissful smile. 'But it's a lovely match.'

Suddenly she was shaken by a fierce joy that had in it a touch of inexplicable anguish. She crossed her arms over her chest and closed her eyes, racked by the strength of her feelings. 'Oh, Heather,' she whispered, 'it's such a lovely, lovely match.'

CHAPTER FOUR

THE wedding day was bright and glorious. A stream of cars departed from the Residenza, taking the multitude of guests to Palermo Cathedral, and finally, Lorenzo the groom and Bernardo his best man. Only Renato remained, to give the bride away.

The bride was beautiful and the bridesmaid too. Angie's gown was a cream silk of deceptive simplicity. Against it her skin glowed warmly, and her deep blue eyes sparkled. Heather saw that sparkle and read it correctly.

'I believe some Sicilian wedding customs are the same as those in England,' she teased. 'Like the one about the bridesmaid and the best man.'

Angie had barely seen Bernardo since they'd parted the night before last. He'd appeared at the Residenza yesterday, but spent his time with his brothers in last-minute preparations, before the three of them had gone out for a stag supper.

The women had an early night, but Angie wandered out onto the terrace in the early hours and saw them arriving home. She hoped Bernardo would look up and see her, and when he didn't she began to understand how intolerable the day had been without him. There were so many hours until she would see him in the cathedral.

Now the hours had narrowed down to a few minutes, and already her heart was beating in anticipation.

Slowly they walked downstairs to where the car was waiting. Heather and Angie climbed into the back and when Renato had joined them they were ready to go.

Angie spent the short journey admiring Heather. That was how a bride ought to look, she thought: beautiful and glorious, glowing with happiness on her way to marry the man she adored. And he would be there at the altar waiting for her, gazing back down the aisle, watching his bride approach.

Bernardo would also be there today, at the groom's side. But he wouldn't be watching the bride. Angie knew that. He would have eyes only for herself. He might even give her one of the quiet, grave smiles that made her heart turn over. She would smile back, just a little, and the onlookers would see them and exchange knowing looks, for it was well known that one wedding sowed the seeds for another.

Then she wondered at herself. For it had been no part of her plan to leave her successful career in her own country, and come to live here for good. Yet it was either that or leave Bernardo, and her heart cried out at the thought. Only a few days ago she'd called him her match and, whatever it cost her, there was no turning back now.

She thought of her other romances, short-lived bursts of thrilling emotion, from which she'd escaped before danger threatened. But danger had threatened from the first moment of their meeting, and she hadn't even tried to escape.

When the car stopped Heather stood while Angie adjusted her dress and veil to perfection, before walking into the Cathedral on Renato's arm, Angie a few steps behind them. The dim light inside made her blink a little after bright sunshine. The organ pealed out in triumph as they prepared to start the journey down the aisle.

But something was wrong. Bernardo was hurrying towards them, frowning, saying that Lorenzo had vanished. Angie could hardly take in the monstrous words. This couldn't be happening. Any moment now Lorenzo would appear to claim his bride.

But he didn't appear. Instead, a teenage boy hurried in, thrust a paper into Heather's bridal bouquet, and ran.

Angie watched as Heather opened the paper and read what Lorenzo had written. She saw her friend's cheeks turn deadly pale, and she moved to where she could read it over her shoulder. Stripped to its essentials the letter said that he had never really wanted this marriage, but Renato had pushed him into it. They were terrible words for a bride to read on her wedding day.

Bernardo too had contrived to read it, and when Angie looked into his face she saw something that alarmed her. For a brief moment this wasn't a civilised man, but a primitive force, a Sicilian, facing a situation that called for blood.

Baptista had joined them and was listening, pale and distraught. As it dawned on her that her son had abandoned his bride she covered her eyes with her hand and swayed. Renato caught her just in time.

'Lie her down,' Angie said quickly, tossing her bouquet aside and becoming all doctor. She knelt beside the old woman and felt her heart, frowning.

'Is it a heart attack?' Renato asked tensely, kneeling on the other side.

'I don't think so, but she needs to get to the hospital.'

His response was to lift his mother in his arms and stride to the door, followed by Bernardo. 'The hospital is close. We'll go straight there.'

He raced out to the first of the waiting cars. Angie and Heather took the next one. By the time they reached the hospital Baptista had already been whisked away and the brothers were pacing the corridor.

Beneath Bernardo's calm she could sense the tension,

and she remembered his ambivalent relationship with
Baptista, how affection and resentment seemed to be
mixed in his feelings for her. She could guess how that
must be torturing him now, and she squeezed his hand,
trying to reassure him.

Heather looked down at her bridal glory which now
seemed like a sick joke. She was pale but very calm as
she asked Bernardo to call the Residenza and get
Baptista's maid to bring some day clothes for them. In
half an hour the maid arrived and they were able to
change.

The two men were allowed in to see Baptista. Then
Heather was summoned in, leaving Angie to walk the corridor restlessly, until her friend emerged, looking more
desperate than ever.

'What is it?' Angie asked, alarmed.

'I just hoped to get out of here, but Baptista wants me
to stay. I had to promise her, she's so ill. But how do I
live in the same house with Renato without telling him
how much I hate him?'

Renato, Angie noticed. Not Lorenzo.

Suddenly she wanted Bernardo's arms around her more
than anything in the world.

The Residenza was like a ghost house. The guests had
gone, the day was over, and everywhere was in darkness.

Heather had slipped away to be alone, and Angie took
refuge in the garden. Until now Baptista's illness and the
need to support her friend had kept her calm and controlled, but now she was more blazingly angry than she'd
ever been in her life. She wanted to cry, she wanted to
rage against the silver moon that hung so indifferently in
the sky. She walked stormily up and down the flagstone
paths, bitter against the whole Martelli family.

'Angie—' Bernardo's voice said from the shadows.

She flung him a look and continued pacing.

'I know what you must feel—how badly you must think of us.'

'You can't imagine what I'm thinking,' she said fiercely. 'If I had Lorenzo here I'd—I'd—how could he do it? How could he expose her to that? Did you see her face?'

'Yes, and I'm ashamed for my brother. Don't think I excuse him.'

'You couldn't, could you? Nobody could excuse that cheap, cowardly—'

'But I think Renato has also been to blame for pushing the marriage too hard.'

'Oh, yes, that fits!' Angie said explosively. 'I've never liked Renato. Now I think I hate them both equally.'

'Darling, don't pace about like that.' Trying to calm her, he reached out, but she thrust him aside.

'Don't come near me,' she warned. 'I'm not safe. I'd like to commit murder. Pacing about is only a substitute.'

He managed to take hold of her, trying to look into her face. She turned bitter, smouldering eyes on him and he was startled. He'd been enchanted by her dainty looks and sunny temper, and impressed by her skills when she tended the little girl. But it hadn't occurred to him that she had a core of steel.

'Don't talk about hating,' he begged. 'Not you.'

'I can't help it. I've never hated anyone before and I don't know how to stop. Heather's nothing, isn't she? Just a stranger from another country who can be treated any old way—'

'That's not fair. We've welcomed her, made much of her—'

'And then the whole pack of you gathered together to watch her being humiliated,' she raged.

He tightened his grip, giving her shoulders a little shake. 'And so the whole pack of us are tarred with the same brush?' he demanded harshly. 'Is that what you're saying? Do you hate all of us—every one?'

The question brought her up short. She pressed her lips together, trying to keep back tears of anger, and shook her head.

'Oh, stop being so reasonable,' she said wretchedly. 'I'm not thinking straight or talking straight. Don't take any notice, just—just let me go.'

'Never in life,' he said, tightening his arms and bending his head.

At first she stiffened, too angry to be kissed. But his lips had the effect of calming anger, and he wouldn't let her refuse. He was determined to make her forget everything but himself. 'Don't hate me,' he whispered.

'I don't—not you—it's just—' Explanations were lost in the excitement that he could induce so easily. What else mattered but this? She clung to him, caring only for the fact that they were here alone together. It seemed so long since the night he'd almost made love to her, and she'd longed for him so much. Now a sweet comfort was beginning to pervade her, as though his very touch could make the world right.

He caressed her face gently. 'Hush—hush—forget the others. Think only of us. I thought you looked beautiful today.'

'I hoped you'd like me.'

'Like? Do you think that's all I feel for you? There's so much to say, but I can't say it here or now. As soon as Baptista's better I shall return to Montedoro. I want you to come with me.'

'How can I leave Heather?'

'Darling, she's strong. Let her confront the family in her own way. You can't do it for her. Come with me to the place where we belong together, and there will be only us.'

'Yes,' she said joyfully. 'Oh, yes…'

'And perhaps when we're there, I shall manage to say how much I love you. I wonder if there is a way. But I will try.'

'Tell me now,' Angie begged.

'I am not skilled with words,' he said humbly. 'I can't tell you what you are in my life, only that you are my life. You are every part of it. We've known each other such a little time, yet I think of you as soon as I wake up in the morning and I go to sleep holding you in my heart. You are there in my dreams. All this and more I will tell you, when we are safe in the place that I long to make our home.'

They slipped quietly back into the house. The lights were low and there was nobody to see them as he led her, hand in hand, up the stairs to her door.

'I shall stay here tonight,' he said, 'and we'll leave tomorrow early. Goodnight.' He kissed her gently, but through the gentleness she could feel the tumult inside him, matching her own.

'Goodnight,' he whispered again, and left her.

Angie slipped into her own room and found it empty. She wondered where Heather was, and if she should go and look for her, but her friend arrived a moment later. She looked pale and drawn, but composed.

'Are you all right?' Angie asked anxiously.

'Yes, I'm fine really. I've been fighting with Renato.' She sounded numb, as though all feeling had died in her.

'I suppose there's only him to fight since Lorenzo took care to get out of range,' Angie said bitterly.

'Don't blame Lorenzo,' Heather said unexpectedly. 'I've learned a few things from Renato tonight.' Her eyes kindled. 'He didn't like admitting it, but I forced it out of him.'

'Admitting what?' Angie asked.

'It seems that Lorenzo tried to be honest with me days ago. That's why he came back from Stockholm early, to tell me he was having doubts and wanted to postpone the wedding. And Renato stopped him. Can you believe that? He even told him I'd been jilted before, so of course Lorenzo felt it was his duty to go through with it.'

'I could strangle Renato,' Angie said fiercely.

'Join the queue. If there's one good thing to come out of this, it's that I won't have to be related to him. Oh, I can't think about it any more tonight. I'm so tired, my mind's shutting down.'

'Will you need me tomorrow?'

Heather smiled in quick understanding. 'No, I'm fine. You spend the day with Bernardo.' Heather smiled and threw her arms about her friend in a sudden burst of emotion. 'Darling, I'm so glad for you! At least one of us is going to have a happy ending.'

Although Angie had some qualms about leaving Heather she soon realised that Bernardo had been right when he said her friend needed to find her own way through this. For the first time she understood Heather's inner strength. When Lorenzo crept back home she didn't flinch from their meeting, confronting him with a cool dignity and even a touch of humour that made him ashamed. This she learned from Bernardo, who saw Lorenzo straight afterwards.

Heather was there too when Baptista returned from hospital, much recovered. Despite what had happened the old woman still clung to her as a daughter, and refused to accept back the gift of Bella Rosaria.

'They're very alike in many ways,' Bernardo told Angie. 'Heather has both my brothers creeping around her on hot coals. They can't make her out, and it puzzles them. Do them both good. I can see why Baptista likes having her here.'

Angie and Bernardo spent as much time as they could together, growing closer, relishing the sweet understanding that was developing between them. Angie began to see why Baptista said he lived as a relatively poor man. In contrast to the armies of servants at the Residenza, he had only Stella who cleaned the house and did some, but not all of the cooking. Some meals he made for himself, and insisted on her trying them, watching with a touching anxiety until she said they were delicious. His home was frugal to the point of austerity. The only modern comfort was central heating which, he assured her, the bleak winters made vital.

Once he'd spoken of this place as their future home, but after that he made no formal suggestion of marriage. Yet she noticed that he frequently offered these explanations, as though he felt a duty to make everything clear to her.

She thought she understood. It wouldn't be the comfortable life she was used to, but neither was his dwelling the bleak, impoverished hovel that he seemed determined to paint.

Once he said, 'I wish it was winter now and you could see for yourself how unpleasant it is—it can't be described—'

'Darling—' she stroked his face gently '—there's no need for this.'

It made her heart ache to see how just her touch and a few words could bring him peace. She knew that he loved her, but it was his need that set the seal on it. She didn't know what the years ahead might bring, but she was sure nothing could separate them now. They clung together, arms tightly wound around each other, exchanging warmth and reassurance.

'Let's have a picnic this afternoon,' he said at last. 'On a day like this, we should be out.'

'Lovely.'

'I'll make us some snacks.'

'While you're doing that, can I use your computer to get onto the net?'

'Of course. I'll log on for you.' He typed in his password, pulled out the chair for her and said, 'I'll bring you some coffee.'

Angie called up her father's web site and emailed him through it. Then she browsed through the site, checking out his latest updates. Dr Harvey Wendham was proud of his site, which he maintained himself, almost as proud as he was of the luxurious Harley Street clinic it advertised.

'The old devil,' she chuckled. 'He doesn't stint himself.'

He was a well-known plastic surgeon whose patients included several film stars and the occasional top-ranking politician, prepared to pay over the odds for his total discretion as much as for his skill. For years he'd worked at the lower-paid end of the medical profession, 'putting in his time' as he called it, but now he'd struck gold and was enjoying it.

Angie knew that he was disappointed that neither of her brothers had joined him in the clinic, and was hoping that she, his youngest child, would make good their deficiencies. But she'd hesitated. She had several other job offers, some attractive, some offering little more than hard work and low pay, plus a lot of satisfaction.

Now all her plans seemed to have been made for her. She loved Bernardo and he loved her. How could she ever think of leaving him?

'Coffee for *la signora*,' Bernardo carolled, pushing open the door and carrying in a tray with two cups and a pot of coffee.

'Oh, lovely!' She began pouring while he looked at the screen over her shoulder.

'What's the matter?' she asked, for he'd muttered something she didn't understand, but which sounded both disbelieving and contemptuous.

'This fellow who calls himself a doctor, when he cares nothing for the sick, only lining his own pocket.'

'He's supposed to be very good at what he does,' Angie observed, enjoying the thought of Bernardo's face when he learned the truth. Her father's name wasn't visible onscreen at the moment. She settled back to relish the joke.

'And what does he do?' Bernardo said derisively. 'While there are people in the world with real needs, he does cosmetic surgery, to make himself money. He has a gift that comes from God, and he used it to make himself a million.'

'Several million actually, but a lot of that—'

She was about to say that much of it was given to charity but Bernardo was in full spate. 'Several million, because he's a man who must have money.'

'He also does a lot of good,' Angie said, beginning to be cross. 'It's not just film stars. It's disfigured children. He happens to be my father, and I'll thank you not to abuse him.'

He looked at her strangely. 'This man is your father?'

Angie flicked back to a previous page, showing her father's name: Dr Harvey Wendham, then glanced at Bernardo's face, expecting to see him look rueful and uncomfortable. Then they could laugh together.

But he looked as if someone had given him a savage blow over the heart.

'Bernardo—what is it? You look ill.'

'Nothing—nothing,' he recovered himself quickly, and smiled. But it was a painful smile, as though he were dying inside.

'What is it?' she begged, suddenly scared.

'I just hadn't realised—that you came from a wealthy family.'

She shrugged. 'All right, we're well off but—'

'Your father is a multi-millionaire.'

'Does it matter?'

'I suppose not—it *shouldn't* matter.'

'No, it shouldn't. I'm still me.'

'I thought you were poor,' he burst out. 'You and Heather—'

'Heather's always been as poor as a church mouse.'

'But you share a home.'

'We're friends. The house belongs to me. I rent her space in it because I like her company. It's never come between us.'

'And this house—it wouldn't happen to be in the wealthiest part of London, would it?'

'It's in Mayfair, yes. So what?'

'So what?' he echoed in a shaking voice. 'So I've been living in a fool's paradise.'

The flicker of alarm inside her was growing higher, resisting her attempts to quench it. This wasn't something that could just be laughed aside, after all.

'You don't mean this makes a difference to us?' she demanded, trying to keep it light. 'Why should it? I'm not some spoilt brat. I'm a hard-working and very tough professional woman. That hasn't changed.'

'No, it hasn't,' he said in a voice that was just a little too decided, as though he were trying to reassure himself. 'You are still Angie, still the woman I love. Nothing can change that. After all, it's your father who is rich, not you.'

She drew a slow breath and turned away, so that he shouldn't see the indecision in her face. She ought to tell him now that her father had settled a million on her the year before, but she knew, with terrified certainty, that it would be a dangerous admission to make to this man whose face had suddenly become so aloof.

She would tell him one day, of course she would. One day soon. But surely she could wait just a little, until he was ready to hear?

They went on the planned picnic, smiling and talking brightly as though nothing had happened: as though pretending could undo the damage.

He drove her down the mountain a short way, stopping at the spot where they had shared their first kiss.

'This is the perfect place,' she said. 'Remember when we were here before?'

She heard the unease in her own voice and knew that he'd heard it too. How futile to recall a time that had gone. Even though it was just a few days ago, that moment, with its happiness, was already far in the past.

Their efforts to sound normal only made things worse. Something destructive had happened, but she still couldn't make herself believe it was a serious threat to their love.

What did money matter? But the churning unease inside her wouldn't be calmed.

They ate the picnic, determinedly cheerful. Once Angie tried to raise the dangerous subject, but he side-stepped it neatly. At last silence fell between them. Angie looked around and found saw him lying back in the grass, one hand behind his head. Smiling, she leaned over him, and saw that he was asleep.

'All right,' she whispered. 'When you wake up it will seem better.'

But when he awoke it wasn't better. He looked at her with remote eyes, and she realised, with terror, that she didn't know how to bridge the widening gap between them.

CHAPTER FIVE

A SLEEPLESS night left her feeling no better, and when Bernardo arrived at the Residenza early something in his face told her that things were worse. He regarded her with a cold, bitter, unfriendliness that she had thought never to see from him.

'I wonder when you would have told me,' he said quietly.

'Told you what?' she asked, although her fear was rising.

'Yesterday I said that it was your father who was rich, not you. Why didn't you tell me about the million he gave you?'

Dear God! she thought. *Not like this. Please, not like this.*

'Because I couldn't,' she said desperately. 'You were so worked up about his having money at all, I couldn't make it worse. I would have told you, when we'd sorted this out, and you were ready to hear. How did you know?'

'From the internet. I searched for your father last night. His name cropped up a good deal, especially on one site called Socialite Doctors. It had links to everything that's ever been written about him. That's how I found this.' He spread out some pages on the table. 'I printed it out.'

With dismay she recognised an article that had appeared a few months earlier. Her father, innocently proud of his new home set in extensive leafy grounds, had taken the journalist on a guided tour of its luxuries.

There was herself, described as 'By day a dedicated

70

doctor, by night, a girl who knows how to party.' The picture showed her dancing a wild rumba in a revealing dress, her head thrown back in enjoyment. Enough of the background could be seen to show that this was a night-club, the kind of place where the rich hung out, and only the very best champagne was served.

More pictures. Herself at the wheel of the car that was her pride and joy, and that nobody living on a doctor's salary could have afforded. And her home in the most expensive part of London.

'All this time,' he said heavily, 'you never told me.'

'I wasn't deceiving you. It just didn't occur to me that it was an issue.'

'But you deceived me yesterday about the money your father settled on you. I wonder how long you would have concealed the truth. And how much—or how little—you would have told me.'

'You make it sound as though I had something to be ashamed of,' she said angrily. 'I haven't committed a crime by being rich.'

'No, you haven't. But you should have been honest with me, and not let me fool myself with dreams about making you my wife and the life we might build together.'

'When should I have told you?' she demanded indignantly. 'The day I arrived? Maybe when we met at the airport I should have said, "Keep your distance from me because I'm too rich for you." How could I know it would matter? You're not exactly poor yourself.'

'The Martelli family is wealthy, not me. I've taken from them the bare minimum I felt entitled to, and don't live like a rich man. You know why. I can't change that. It's too deeply a part of me. It would be like throwing away my soul.'

'And I understand that but—'

'You don't begin to understand.' Bernardo was very pale as he added, 'I don't entirely understand it myself. I only know that I *must* live this way. I was going to beg you to marry me. It would have been a hard decision for you, because Montedoro isn't an easy place to live. But I thought you were like myself, used to a tough life, and perhaps, with love, it might be possible.'

'It *is* possible,' she said earnestly. 'You think I don't know about a tough life? I'm a doctor.'

'And at the end of the day you go home to your Mayfair apartment with all its luxuries. You couldn't live at the top of that mountain. You think you could, but you'd find otherwise when it was too late. And what then? You'd want to run away and live in Palermo. Or even England.'

'You have a nice opinion of me,' she said angrily. 'A weakling who doesn't know how to love or give.'

'No, but I know this life, and you don't. I know what you'd be letting yourself in for. You see Montedoro as it is now, in the summer sun, when the tourists are there. But in the winter the tourists go home and the town is swathed in freezing mist that soaks through to your bones. And the winds howl for weeks on end and sap your spirit.'

'Well, would living in Palermo be so bad? It's still Sicily and—' She stopped at the sight of his face. 'Never mind. I shouldn't have said it.'

'I'm glad you did. And you're right. Why shouldn't you live among the comforts you're used to? But I can't do that. There's something in me that I can't overcome. It drives me, it makes me do things I don't want to do. I have to listen to it.'

'All right, so I've got money. So let's use it. Let's spend some on your home and make it really comfortable. And if the winters are rough surely we could come down to Palermo for a few weeks—'

'Living off your money you mean?' he asked, white-faced.

'Well, I've got it, and if it's mine, it's yours.'

'Never!' The word was like a whiplash. 'Take money from you? You really think I'd do that?'

'Why not? These days—'

As soon as she said 'these days', she realised what she was up against. Bernardo wasn't a modern man with a modern attitude to women. He was a man with a soul in turmoil, whose absorption into a rich family had embittered him once, and who would fight like the devil to stop it happening again.

But even with the inevitable staring her in the face, she wouldn't admit it. Not yet. She too knew how to fight, and her love was worth fighting for.

'We've got to find a way around this,' she said, trying to sound firm. 'We've got something special. We can't just give it up.'

'If we were married it would lead to misery,' he said wretchedly. 'I can't take money from you, and you can't live without it. One day you'd go back to England to visit your family, and you wouldn't return. And I—' He shuddered.

'What would you do?' she whispered.

There was a long pause before he answered, and then she could hardly make out his words. 'I think I might follow you.'

She misunderstood him and for a moment relief flooded her. 'Well, then, if you—'

'Don't you understand?' he demanded fiercely. 'That's how much I love you, enough to stop being a man and become a beaten dog, trailing after you, begging you to let me stay with you on any terms. I might turn my back on those who need me, and try to lead your life, hating and despising myself more with every day.'

Angie paled. 'Do you really think I'd let that happen?' she asked. 'Do you think I'd want you to be less than a man, on your terms. If that's so, it's no wonder you're ashamed of loving me.'

'I'm not—'

'But you are,' she said, her temper rising. 'Don't you realise, that's exactly what you've just revealed? You say "that's how much I love you", but to you love means being a beaten dog, because you equate it with giving in to a woman, and you're so arrogant that you don't really think any woman is worth it. Why do you love me if you despise me too? Or is it only because I've got money you despise me?'

'Don't say that,' he begged hoarsely. 'That isn't what I—'

'It's not what you meant to say, but it came through. You want to love me just so much and no more, counting every grain to see if you've given me more than you think I deserve. That's not what I understand by love. I'd have given up everything to be here with you, and been proud of loving a man who was worth the sacrifice. But you—'

'Don't!' he said fiercely. 'Don't say any more.'

'I wasn't going to. What else is there to say?'

She turned and ran out of the house. For the next hour she walked the streets, trying to believe that this was really happening. But of course, it wasn't. It was a bad dream, and when she returned she would find him there, smiling at her. She would go into his arms and they would plan their lives together.

But when she returned to the Residenza and saw him watching anxiously for her she knew, with a sinking heart, that nothing had changed. He was doing something that tore him apart, but he would do it anyway. Because he was the man he was, and he could do nothing else.

She ran into his arms, which opened for her, then closed tighter than ever.

'I'm sorry for what I said,' she whispered.

'Say what you like of me,' he said huskily. 'But try not to hate me, and understand that I have no choice.'

There was no longer anything to stay for. Heather was remaining in Sicily at Baptista's insistence, so Angie made one reservation on the flight from Palermo to London. Bernardo took her to the airport, and they waited in sad silence for her flight to be called. It was like being at a funeral.

At last it was time for her to go to the Departure Lounge, where he couldn't follow.

'Forgive me,' he said huskily. 'I would break the barrier down if I could, but it's stronger than I am. I still love you. I will never love another woman. But I have no power against this thing.'

She didn't answer in words. But she put her hand up against his cheek, watching him with eyes that were gentle and tender. He placed his own hand over hers, and turned his head so that his lips were against her palm. She had called him arrogant, but he didn't look arrogant now. Rather he seemed ill and crushed by his agony, as though all his strength had gone. With another man she might have hoped that he would yield at the last moment. But she knew that Bernardo had never been further from yielding. However beaten down he seemed, the core of the man remained steely strong and stubborn.

'Bernardo—' she whispered.

'Go,' he begged. 'Go before my heart breaks.'

* * *

Angie had deferred a decision on several job offers until she returned to England, meaning to consider them at leisure. But within an hour of landing she had accepted work at her father's clinic, for no other reason than that she could start at once. The thought of spending time at home with nothing to do was intolerable.

It was a good decision. The work at the Wendham Clinic was far more demanding than anyone would have thought who looked only at its well known patients and sky high costs. Harvey Wendham was a brilliant surgeon who'd made his reputation by being the best in his field. He set about training his daughter as his assistant, and his demands filled her life.

But there were still too many evenings with no distraction, and gradually her work at the clinic ceased to act as a charm against misery. She soon mastered it, and as the demands grew, so did her skill. Her father was delighted. Her brothers congratulated her. In the midst of success she felt lost in a dreary desert.

As always, she had no shortage of admirers. Most of them she refused, but she allowed one man to buy her dinner, and another to take her dancing. They had all the social graces that Bernardo lacked, plus smooth tongues that prevented them ever saying the wrong thing. At one time she would have been charmed by them, if only briefly. Now she kept comparing them, to their disadvantage, to a man with no company skills, who said only what he thought, even if it offended people. After one date she never saw either of them again.

Everything she did seemed pointless, even, sometimes, her work. She gave it her best shot, because that was her way, but there was no sense of satisfaction to help her bear her sadness, no fulfilment to blot out Bernardo's torturing image.

At first she'd hoped that Heather would follow her soon, but through telephone calls she followed the incredible story that was happening in Sicily. To everyone's amazement Baptista had come up with her own solution to the mess—an arranged marriage, with—

'*Renato?*' Angie echoed, aghast. 'It's a bad joke. You can't stand him.'

'That's what I told her,' Heather said. 'I said all I wanted was to kick his shins. She says when we're married I can do it every day.'

Angie gave an unwilling laugh. 'You've got to hand it to Baptista. She's like no other woman.'

'The way she sees it, her family has insulted me, and must make amends.'

'But that's medieval.'

'These people are Sicilians, Angie. They're not like us. In fact, they're not like anyone else in the world. There *is* something medieval about them. They believe that there's a right way to do things. In a sense you've got to admire them for it, even if some of the things they think right seem incomprehensible to us.'

'Oh, yes,' Angie sighed. 'I know that.'

To escape Baptista's matchmaking, Heather moved into Bella Rosaria. Angie had a vision of her living there alone, like a mysterious lady in a tower, while her suitors prowled around outside. But it wouldn't last. Some day soon Heather would return to England, and at least she would have some friendly company in the intolerable emptiness of her life.

But instead, the phone rang one evening, and it was Heather, with the incredible news that she had agreed to the marriage. 'And I'd like you to be my bridesmaid. Can you get away?'

'Yes, I'm sure I can.' She could hardly breathe enough to ask the next question. 'Heather—does Bernardo—?'

'He doesn't know I'm asking you, and I'm not going to tell him.'

'But is he—?'

'He's very unhappy. It could be just the right moment for you to come back.'

When she'd hung up Angie threw herself back on the sofa, her hands over her face, and gave herself up to longing. To see Bernardo again, to hear his voice and perhaps feel his arms about her. It might not be wise to take him by surprise, but she was powerless to refuse. She discovered that she was crying, which was absurd. She was happier than she'd been for weeks, but it was a bittersweet kind of happiness that carried the promise of more grief.

Stop being ridiculous, she told herself sternly. She who dares, wins! And I'm going to dare!

When she asked for the time off her father took one look at her pale face and granted it. She flew into Palermo Airport the evening before the wedding and found Heather waiting for her.

'Bernardo's still in Montedoro,' she said. 'He won't be down until early tomorrow morning. But we'll eat out and slip into the house later by a side door so that none of the servants see you.'

Over supper in a little restaurant Heather tried to explain why she was marrying a man she'd always seemed to dislike.

'Baptista arranged everything,' she said. 'She's determined to keep me in the family. She even gave me her estate of Bella Rosaria, to be my dowry for Lorenzo, and when we broke up she wouldn't take it back. I have to marry him to return it to the family.'

'What's Renato's angle?'

'He's getting Bella Rosaria back, which he wants.'

'And?' Angie asked, regarding her sceptically.

'And—and I belong in Sicily. I've loved this place since the day we arrived, and this seems the best way to stay.'

'Phooey!' Angie said with sudden enlightenment. 'You and Renato are in love.'

'Nobody could be in love with Renato,' Heather said firmly. 'Marriage will just make it more convenient for fighting with him.'

'OK, you're going to have a stormy marriage.'

'I'll say!' Heather said darkly, but she was laughing.

'But it'll be a happy one, because you *are* in love. That's why you've been at each other's throats since the start.'

'Well, maybe.'

'What about Lorenzo? Doesn't he find the whole situation rather embarrassing?'

Heather smiled. 'I don't think anything could embarrass that young man. Our marriage wouldn't have worked and we both know it. I'm good friends with my "little brother" now.'

They drove back to the Residenza and managed to get into the house without being seen, hurrying silently upstairs to their old room.

'Bernardo really hasn't suspected?' Angie asked as she prepared for bed.

'Not a thing. The first he'll know is when he sees you walking down the aisle with me tomorrow. He's retreated into his eagle's nest and stays there. If Renato needs to talk work he calls him on the phone, or goes up there. I've been living at Bella Rosaria, and he drops in sometimes. He says it's to see if there's anything he can do for me, but he always manages to bring the conversation around to you. I tell him what's happening to you and he drinks it in.'

'Did you tell him I was working for my father now?'

'Yes. Shouldn't I?'

'It's not a state secret. It's just that I can guess what he made of it.'

'He's in a bad way, thin and miserable. Like you.'

'I've been working hard,' Angie said quickly.

'So's he,' Heather said, adding wisely, 'and it doesn't seem to solve the problem for either of you.'

They went to bed, but Angie couldn't sleep. At last she got up, pulled on a wrap and went out onto the terrace, her heart aching as she remembered that this was where she'd stood on the first evening and glanced up to see Bernardo looking down at her. Now there was only an empty space because he preferred to shun company.

She turned to gaze up at the mountains. Somewhere up there was Montedoro and the man she loved, brooding in terrible silence, and thinking of her with his heart. She knew that, because it was the same with her. She was pervaded by a bittersweet joy at being near to him again. She wouldn't think of failure, because it was unthinkable.

Next morning she didn't leave the room until it was time to go to the cathedral with Heather. This time, instead of Renato travelling with them to give the bride away to Lorenzo, a cousin travelled with them to give the bride away to Renato. As before, Bernardo was best man.

The car halted, there was a moment while she straightened the bride's dress, then they were on their way into the cathedral, making their entrance. Her heart beat urgently as she thought of seeing Bernardo again. How would he look when he saw her?

It was a long walk down the aisle, with the choir sing-

ing sweetly, high overhead. Closer and closer—and there
he was, looking more tense and gaunt than when they'd
said goodbye. Was that what their parting had done to
him?

At last he caught sight of her. For a moment nothing
happened except that he froze, motionless. Then a wooden
look came over his face, and he turned to give his attention to the groom. Angie drew in a painful breath. She
couldn't read the brief glimpse she'd had of his face. It
could have meant that he was more glad to see her than
he could cope with, or might could have meant anger,
rejection. The service dragged interminably as she stood
there, looking at his back, wondering if she'd made a
hideous mistake.

Renato slipped the ring on Heather's finger, and she
became his wife. The most incredible marriage in history,
Angie thought. Two people who never had a good word
to say for each other, but they were in love, even if they
hadn't admitted it. And yet she and Bernardo, for whom
love should have been so simple, had somehow made a
mess of it.

The service was over. The organ pealed out overhead
as the bride and groom began the return journey up the
aisle. Angie fell into place behind them with her head up.
Bernardo walked beside her, apparently oblivious of her
but actually as aware of her as she was of him.

On the journey home they shared a car, alone. At last,
she thought, a chance to talk. Seize it before it slipped
away. 'We're you expecting me?' she asked.

He took her hand gently between his. 'I suppose I
was—in a way. I did wonder if Heather would bring you
over.'

'You could have asked her.'

He shook his head and she realised that he would never

have asked. That would be to give something away and, for this most private man, it would be impossible.

He'd pulled himself together, and was managing a fair imitation of polite indifference. 'It's good to see you. I've wondered how you were, and whether all was well with you.'

'And do you think all has been well with me?' she whispered.

'I've never seen you look more beautiful.'

It was true. Her silk dress was of the palest yellow and simply cut to drape softly about her. A coronet of flowers adorned her hair, and her only jewels were pearls nestling against her ears. For a moment he feasted his eyes on her, full of a longing he couldn't hide.

But it was only for a moment. Then he gave a brief smile, and she knew that behind it the shutters had come down again. But she'd seen past his guard. They couldn't go back on that. She knew now. Hope rose in her.

At the reception they sat together. They were on show, and there was little chance to talk of what concerned them, but before the speeches began he said quietly, 'So you went to work in your father's Harley Street clinic?'

'Yes,' she said defiantly. 'He's a brilliant surgeon. I learn a lot from him.'

'That's good,' he said politely. 'I'm glad you're doing so well.'

Unexpectedly her temper rose. 'Why, you patronising—!'

'Please, I only—'

'I know exactly what you meant by that. You think it's easy work from the "fat cat" end of the market, and all I'm fit for.'

'Must we quarrel when we have so little time?'

'We could have all the time we want—'

She couldn't say more. The toasts and speeches were about to begin. Bernardo did his duty with a speech that contained no jokes but much quiet goodwill, and it went down well.

Then it was time for the dancing. Heather and Renato took the floor, and a murmur went around the guests, how well the bride and groom looked together.

'Angie, it's wonderful to see you again. Come and dance with me.'

She looked up into Lorenzo's laughing face. As Heather had said, he was quite untroubled by a situation that another young man might have found embarrassing. Smiling, she took his hand, but at once another hand reached out to clasp hers and disengage it.

'No,' Bernardo said quietly. 'Sorry, Lorenzo.'

His brother grinned and promptly found another partner. Bernardo tightened his grip on her hand. There was a look in his eyes that went to her heart. She let him draw her onto the dance floor and hold her close. She could feel his body trembling next to hers, and she knew the truth he would have hidden from her. If she'd doubted that he still loved her, she didn't doubt it now. He looked as though the heart had been torn out of him.

She didn't speak. For the moment it was enough to be here with him again, held in his arms.

'You should not have come,' he murmured as they circled the dance floor. 'But I have longed for you.'

'Then why shouldn't I have come?'

'*Because* I have longed for you,' he said with a sigh. 'I can't see you without weakening, and I mustn't weaken.'

'Why must you talk like that? Is it weak to love?'

'It might be weak to yield to love,' he said sombrely.

'*Amor mia,* can't you understand? You're a bird of paradise, and Montedoro is a place only for eagles.'

'But you know so little about me. How do you know I couldn't be an eagle too?'

'Don't—please don't—you can't know what you're saying.'

Yet he was so torn that even as his words rejected her he pulled her closer and her senses swam. The misery in his face hurt her, yet beneath the misery she still sensed a stubbornness that she would have to fight. Suddenly she stopped dancing, seized his hand and began to lead him off the dance floor. She didn't stop until they were outside, under the stars.

'Angie—'

'Shut up and kiss me,' she said, pulling him into her arms.

Through the trembling of his body she could feel that he would have resisted her if he could, but he hadn't strength enough for that. Taking her courage in both hands she built on her advantage, kissing him in the ways that he loved, the ways that would call their brief happiness back.

'You can't say goodbye to me again,' she murmured.

'Angie don't do this—don't destroy me—'

'I'm trying to stop you destroying us both. You want me, don't you?'

'You know I want you.'

'Enough to take my hand and jump into the unknown. That's all it needs, my love, just a little courage.'

Between the words her lips were sending him other messages of incitement and delight, torturing him with bliss held just out of reach, driving him crazy. With triumph she sensed that he couldn't hold out against her. She felt his hands in her hair, tearing down the pretty confection that the hairdresser had achieved, so that it fell wildly about her bare shoulders, and his lips followed it, leaving a burning trail against her skin.

'Don't tempt me—' he whispered. 'Sorceress—I'll fight you—'

'I'll tempt you until you're brave enough to take any risk with me. If we can't live in each other's worlds we'll make our own.'

'Don't—' he said hoarsely.

'Yes, my love, take the chance and jump from the highest point of Montedoro, and we'll fly like eagles together.'

'It's crazy—mad—'

'Don't think about that. Haven't you wanted me to kiss you like this?'

'More than anything in life—but it changes nothing—'

'It changes everything,' she said, her lips against his. 'You're mine. You belong to me as I belong to you, and I won't let you go. I don't care what the difficulties are.' To desire was suddenly added anger. She seized his shoulders and shook him, her blazing eyes staring into his. 'We love each other. Doesn't that count for anything?'

'Perhaps it counts for less than you think,' he forced himself to say. 'Must love be the whole of life? Must it matter more than anything else in the world?'

'If it's strong enough—yes,' she said fiercely.

'Do you think I don't love you? Do you think I haven't lain awake night after night, thinking of you, longing for you, telling myself the world would be well lost if only I could make love with you, just once?'

'Then make love to me—now—my room's near—no more questions or decisions—'

'But with the dawn I regained my sanity. It's easy to talk of the world well lost, but it never *is* lost. It stays there, devastated by one foolish action, and we have to live with the consequences of what we've done. How quickly do you think we'd come to hate each other if we tried to live together? You couldn't live my life and I couldn't live yours. We'd destroy each other. *Why can't you see that?*'

'Because you're everything to me,' she cried in passionate anger. 'And maybe love has made me stupid—stupid enough to believe we can make anything possible if we love enough. But I'd rather be my kind of stupid than yours, believing nothing is possible and love isn't worth fighting for.'

Suddenly she saw that all her arts, all her passion and determination had achieved nothing. The agonising sensation of her own heart breaking made her step back sharply, repulsing him with a gesture that was almost a blow.

'If it means so little to you, then maybe it *isn't* worth fighting for,' she cried. 'Maybe I belong back in my old life, but only because you won't grant me the dignity of making my own decisions, even when they're hard. Perhaps we would destroy each other, not for the reason you think, but because I couldn't live with a man who's hard, judgemental, and thinks I need him to tell me what to do.

'Goodbye, Bernardo. I thought I'd made a mistake in coming here, but now I'm glad. It'll save me indulging in regrets.'

Midnight on the terrace. The house was silent. Far out, the moon was reflected on a tranquil sea. Angie stood looking, trying to imprint the scene on her memory, knowing this was the last time she would ever be here.

'So he was as much of a stubborn fool as always?' came Baptista's ironic voice from the shadows.

'Yes,' Angie said bitterly. 'I thought if he'd missed me

as I've missed him, it might change things. But nothing changes.'

'No, nothing changes with Bernardo, and it never will change. He'll love you all his life, and he'll suffer for it so dreadfully that it hurts me to think of.'

'What about my suffering?' Angie asked wryly.

'My dear, I know you are in pain, but you will survive, and you will love again—perhaps not as you love him, but enough. You are warm and open-hearted. You know how to embrace life.

'But Bernardo—' Baptista sighed '—none of this is true of him. He is a hard man, even a harsh one, who doesn't know how to compromise. He conceals himself, even from himself. One woman—just one—found the way to tempt him out into the sunlight, and if he loses her, I don't think he'll ever find the way out again. Think of his life as it will be then. How cold and stunted it will be, and finally how twisted.'

'I know,' Angie whispered huskily. 'When I think of him alone up there, and how happy we could be if only—' She pressed her lips together, but she couldn't stop the tears pouring down her face. 'He thinks I'm only a bird of paradise,' she said, and the cry broke from her, *'but I wanted to be an eagle.'*

'Then be an eagle,' Baptista said trenchantly.

'How can I if he won't let me?'

'Let?' Baptista's voice was scathing. 'Are you that kind of woman, the kind who waits for a man to "let" her? I expected better from you. Do what you believe in. Don't ask his permission. Weak women say, "if only". Strong ones make it happen.'

'Do you think I don't long to make it happen?' she demanded. 'I don't know the way.'

'But I do,' Baptista said, 'and I'm going to show it to you.'

CHAPTER SIX

IN WINTER Montedoro was a ghostly, deserted place, swathed in mist. Now the boutiques were closed and most of the cafés. Feet echoed on the cobbles and all the colour seemed to have drained away, leaving only grey behind.

With the tourists gone, little more than six hundred people remained, and most of them seemed to have crowded into the narrow street to watch the new arrival. Two vans had drawn up. The front one was disgorging furniture, but not very much, because the new doctor had bought Dr Fortuno's practice, house and furniture, lock, stock and barrel.

The largest item was a bed which, even in its dismembered state, spoke of quality and money. The head and foot were highly polished walnut, the mattress thick and springy. There would be trouble getting it through those narrow doorways, they reckoned. It was big. Too big for one person.

Hmm!

The second van was even more interesting. No furniture this time, but large, shiny metal items that the more knowledgeable guessed were medical equipment. There were murmurs in the crowd.

'Dr Fortuno never had any of that stuff.'

'He was an old man... They say he never read a book after he qualified.'

'So who's this new man?'

'It's a woman.'

'Don't be funny!'

'That's her over there.'

'What, that little thing? She's young enough to be my daughter.'

But, for all her youth and her dainty appearance, the new doctor had an air of authority, and when she offered twenty thousand lire to anyone who would help carry her heavy goods inside there was a rush from men enduring the unemployment of winter. In a short time everything was in place and the vans were able to leave.

More people had pressed through the open door to regard the new doctor, wide-eyed.

'Some of you may remember seeing me here last year,' she told them in Italian. 'Now Dr Fortuno has left and from now on I'm going to be the doctor here.' Angie took a deep breath and looked around the circle of faces that gave nothing away. She was gambling everything, and they would never know how nervous she was.

She showed them around the surgery, explaining the new equipment and what it could do for them. At first she was on tenterhooks, ready to beg them not to touch anything, but nobody tried. They seemed to regard it with awe tinged with fear, and she sensed that this part hadn't gone so well. Their eyes, as they regarded her, were curious, baffled, not unfriendly but not welcoming. She was alien to them.

At last somebody spoke. 'Where's Dr Fortuno?'

'He went to live with his sister in Naples,' Angie said.

'He's not coming back then?'

'No,' Angie said with a sinking heart. 'He's not coming back. Have I shown you—?'

But she'd lost their attention. She felt, rather than heard the silence descend and turned from the machine she'd meant to demonstrate to see that the crowd had parted and everyone was looking at a man who'd just entered.

Bernardo stood in the doorway regarding her with a look of dismay and anger she'd never thought to see on his face. This was the man who loved her, but he wasn't glad to see her. For a moment she flinched, then her head went up. She'd known it wasn't going to be easy.

The little crowd melted away, leaving them alone together, watching each other over the distance of the floor.

'What the devil do you think you're doing?' he demanded at last.

'I'm Dr Fortuno's replacement. I'm surprised the gossip hasn't reached you by now.'

'It reached me as soon as I came through the main gate. But you know what I'm asking you. Why you?'

She faced him. 'Why not?'

'Because you don't belong here.'

'That's for me to say.'

His face closed against her. 'Why do you have to make things harder on both of us? This isn't a place to play games. It's bleak and harsh and it'll crush you in a week.'

'I told you once, I'm a lot tougher than I look.'

'And I told you that this is an old-fashioned place. It's never had a woman doctor, and it's not ready for one. You must leave here.'

'Says who?' she demanded, beginning to be angry.

'I will not allow you to stay. Is that plain enough?'

'Perfectly plain. What isn't so plain is how you're going to get rid of me, seeing as how I've bought the house, and the practice. You may own a good deal of this village, but you don't own this house. Nor do you own the convent.'

'What has the convent got to do with anything?'

'Sister Ignatia is a qualified nurse. She's coming in to help me two mornings a week. The nuns are delighted to have a woman doctor.'

'But how——?' Bernardo ran his hand through his hair and looked around him. 'How did you ever get a license to practise in this country?'

'Because I have excellent qualifications which are completely acceptable over here. The only hurdle was getting the paperwork translated and approved. At every stage there seemed to be a new committee who had to agree, and I know it can take a very long time. One of the officials told me about an English doctor who took two years to get his paperwork approved.'

'Exactly. Then how——?'

'But he didn't have Baptista behind him. First she persuaded Dr Fortuno to go. He'd been wanting to go for some time, apparently, but he couldn't find a buyer. When my paperwork came through she got onto Cousin Enrico who knows someone in the Sicilian regional government, and *he* knew a high-ranking official in Rome, who pulled strings and twisted arms, and the whole thing got done in a couple of months.'

'Baptista,' Bernardo said bitterly. 'Baptista did this.'

'Perhaps she felt I was entitled to prove myself. Because actually, Bernardo, your attitude to me is pretty insulting. You decided I wasn't good enough for you——'

'I never——'

'That's what it amounted to. Not good enough for you, not good enough for your home. Just a bird of paradise who's always had a cosy nest. You dumped that on me, never mind whether it was true. Well, now I'm dumping myself on you, and there isn't a thing you can do about it.

'I'm a good doctor and I'm going to be good for this place. To start with I've imported some very modern medical equipment, the kind of thing I'll swear Dr Fortuno had never heard of, and he certainly couldn't have afforded to buy. But I can, because I've got all that disgraceful money that you think puts me beyond the pale.

'Take a good look at this place and see what my wicked wealth has bought. With Sister Ignatia's help I could even do operations, although I devoutly hope I never have to.'

'And how are you going to communicate with your patients?'

'My Italian is excellent, although most of them speak English. They learned it from the tourists.'

'In Montedoro, yes. But your practice spreads far out, to the farmhouses where they only know Sicilian. What will you do then?'

'I've spent the last three months learning.'

'Three months—?'

'I've been working with a Sicilian coach, several hours a day. She says I'm coming on fast. And if necessary I'll hire someone here to help me.'

'And when the snow comes—?'

'I'll get snow shoes,' she yelled. 'I know there are problems, but there are also answers. Why can't you be a little glad to see me?'

'You know why—'

'I'll tell you what I know,' she said furiously. 'You made a decision. It concerned me, but you didn't involve me. You decided for both of us. Now I'm telling you, it's not on. You *don't* decide for me. And you really have a problem with a woman who won't accept your edict, don't you? Boy, are you a Martelli?'

'Don't say that!' he said harshly.

'I will say it. It's true. If you don't like it, tough!'

Exasperated, he began to look about him at the plain dwelling with its shabby furniture and kitchen equipment that came out of the Ark. 'You're going to live with *this*?' he demanded.

'Not all of it. I'm having a new kitchen delivered soon—and, yes, it *is* going to be top of the range at a very fancy price. Like this.' She threw open the bedroom door to reveal the luxurious bed. 'I can do without my creature comforts if I have to, but why should I have to just because you're pig-headed? I won't be a worse doctor because I sleep soft. Better, in fact. Dr Fortuno might have been better if he hadn't slept on a mattress filled with turnips.'

'Please—*signore—dottore—*'

The interruption came from a girl of sixteen who'd just come in from the street. She smiled shyly at Bernardo who greeted her as Ginetta.

'You can clean the bedroom and make the bed,' Angie told her with a smile. 'You'll find all the new bed linen in those cardboard boxes.'

When the girl had disappeared she explained, 'She's going to do my housework. Apart from paying her money I'm going to talk English to her. The Mother Superior found her for me in the convent school. She's the elder sister of the little girl whose leg I tended.'

'Yes, I know the family,' he said curtly. 'You've evidently gotten everything worked out, and what I think doesn't count?'

'No more than my wishes counted with you. It's a different ball game now, Bernardo. We're playing by my rules.'

'And what is it supposed to achieve? At the end of the day, do I give in and marry you?'

At that, Angie lost her temper, big time.

'Oh, boy, you really fancy yourself, don't you? You think I went to all this trouble because I'm desperate to marry you? What do you think I've been doing recently,

Bernardo? Sitting at home like a wallflower because no other man wants me?'

He regarded her, trying to maintain his distance, reluctantly taking in everything he'd been trying to forget: her dainty figure that had been designed for dancing in costly evening wear, not roughing it in the mountains, her angel face with its halo of flyaway blonde hair.

No wallflower. No sitting at home. He could guess about the men who pursued her, danced with their arms about her, kissed the mouth that had once moved so sweetly against his own. He could, but he didn't dare in case he went mad. He wondered why he'd never noticed something else about that lovely mouth, its sheer mulish obstinacy.

'I never imagined you lonely—' he began.

'Then you're a fool,' she whispered so that he didn't hear. Then, eyes flashing, she took up the argument. 'I did not uproot my life to come all this way because I was desperate for a husband. I have my own reasons. OK, maybe I am as weak and foolish as you think me—'

'I never said—'

'You said a lot more than you think. All sorts of little prejudices came creeping out between the lines. A psychologist could have a field day with what you said, what you didn't say, and what you don't realise you said.

'If I believe you I'm just a weakling who falls apart when the going gets tough. I don't think I am like that, but I want to find out. For *me*, not for you. It has nothing to do with you. In fact, you're surplus to requirements, and I'd be obliged if you'd leave because I have a lot of work to do.'

He stared at her for a moment, and walked out without another word.

*   *   *

Well, I sure picked my time, she thought as she snuggled down in bed that night. Second week in January, just when the weather's taking a nosedive to freezing, where it will stay for at least a month. Any sensible person would have done this in spring, but not me. And Bernardo thinks I'm a weakling.

Bernardo be blowed!

She'd started with a stroke of luck in getting the nuns on her side. Her second lucky break came the following week, during a phone call with Heather, who mentioned an outbreak of flu in Palermo. So far there were no cases in Montedoro and Angie went into action fast. Every nun in the convent was vaccinated; also the local priest, Father Marco, a desperate gossip who 'happened' to be visiting the convent at the time. He was a plump little man in his fifties with a belligerent manner and a kind heart.

He had two hobbies in life, an obsessive interest in boxing, and his running feud with Olivero Donati, who was the mayor of Montedoro, and his own distant cousin. Donati was a meek, nervous little man who enjoyed the ceremonial aspects of being mayor but couldn't say boo to a goose. Father Marco had pulled strings to get him the job, but thereafter felt entitled to sit on him whenever he pleased. Mostly Olivero put up with it, but sometimes he remembered his mayoral dignity and found the courage to speak up. Only to be sat on again.

Within hours of the priest receiving his shot Olivero presented himself at the surgery, declaring it his duty to give a lead to the citizens who looked to him for guidance. Suppressing a grin, Angie praised him for his civic spirit and declared that she wished there were more citizens like him.

In addition every child in the school was sent home with a letter, signed by the Superior, urging all parents to have their children vaccinated, and also themselves. The villagers might be wary of her but they trusted Mother Francesca. The take up was good, but not as complete as she'd hoped. She considered the problem, identified the cause and decided on measures to tackle it.

Bernardo, peacefully eating his supper, was startled by a loud banging on his front door. Stella opened it to admit a short figure of indeterminate gender, so heavily wrapped up that it was almost as broad as it was long.

'*Buona notte, dottore,*' she cried, after recognising the visitor with difficulty. 'Come into the warm and I'll bring you some hot coffee.'

'Thank you, Stella,' Angie said cheerfully. 'I could do with it.'

She threw back the hood of her jacket, disclosing a bright-eyed face, full of smiles. If Bernardo had expected the cold to drive her under he could see his mistake. She was glowing with health and vigour, her cheeks rosy from her exertions.

'Good evening, Signor Tornese,' she said, clasping Bernardo's hand and pumping it vigorously.

'Good evening, *dottore.*' Bernardo's manner was polite but wary.

Stella set a large cup of coffee before her. 'How you like our cold weather, eh?'

'I'm coping. Look at me.' Angie indicated her heavy boots and trousers. 'You know what I'm wearing under this? Red flannel combinations.'

Stella went into gales of laughter.

'No, really, you should try it,' Angie assured her. 'So should you, *signore*. It's a wonderful way to keep warm.'

'Thank you, I am warm enough,' Bernardo said. 'You are welcome, of course—'

'Liar,' she murmured provocatively.

PLAY THE
Lucky Key Game
and get

HOW TO PLAY:

1. With a coin, carefully scratch off gold area at the right. Then check the claim chart to see what we have for you — **2 FREE BOOKS** and a **FREE GIFT** — **ALL YOURS FREE!**

2. Send back the card and you'll receive two brand-new Love Inspired™ novels. These books have a cover price of $4.50 each in the U.S. and $5.25 each in Canada, but they are yours to keep absolutely free.

3. There's no catch. You're under no obligation to buy anything. We charge nothing — ZERO — for your first shipment. And you don't have to make any minimum number of purchases — not even one!

4. The fact is, thousands of readers enjoy receiving books by mail from the Steeple Hill Reader Service™. They enjoy the convenience of home delivery...they like getting the best new novels at discount prices, BEFORE they're available in stores...and they love their *Heart to Heart* subscriber newsletter featuring author news, horoscopes, recipes, book reviews and much more!

5. We hope that after receiving your free books you'll want to remain a subscriber. But the choice is yours — to continue or cancel, any time at all! So why not take us up on our invitation, with no risk of any kind. You'll be glad you did!

YOURS FREE!
A SURPRISE MYSTERY GIFT

We can't tell you what it is...but we're sure you'll like it! A

FREE GIFT—
just for playing the LUCKY KEY game!

Visit us online at
www.eHarlequin.com

FREE GIFTS!

PLAY THE
Lucky Key Game

Scratch gold area with a coin.
Then check below to see the gifts you get!

303 IDL DC6N
103 IDL DC6E

DETACH AND MAIL CARD TODAY!

YES! I have scratched off the gold area. Please send me the 2 Free books and gift for which I qualify. I understand I am under no obligation to purchase any books, as explained on the back and on the opposite page.

NAME   (PLEASE PRINT CLEARLY)

ADDRESS

APT.#   CITY

STATE/PROV.   ZIP/POSTAL CODE

2 free books plus a mystery gift	1 free book
2 free books	Try Again!

(H-R-OS-07/01)

Steeple Hill Reader Service™ — Here's how it works:

Accepting your 2 free books and gift places you under no obligation to buy anything. You may keep the books and gift and return the shipping statement marked "cancel." If you do not cancel, about a month later we'll send you 3 additional novels and bill you just $3.74 each in the U.S., or $3.96 each in Canada, plus 25¢ shipping & handling per book and applicable taxes if any.* That's the complete price and — compared to cover prices of $4.50 each in the U.S. and $5.25 each in Canada — it's quite a bargain! You may cancel at any time, but if you choose to continue, every month we'll send you 3 more books, which you may either purchase at the discount price or return to us and cancel your subscription.

*Terms and prices subject to change without notice. Sales tax applicable in N.Y. Canadian residents will be charged applicable provincial taxes and GST.

If offer card is missing write to: Steeple Hill Reader Service, 3010 Walden Ave., P.O. Box 1867, Buffalo NY 14240-1867

BUSINESS REPLY MAIL
FIRST-CLASS MAIL   PERMIT NO. 717-003   BUFFALO, NY

POSTAGE WILL BE PAID BY ADDRESSEE

STEEPLE HILL READER SERVICE
3010 WALDEN AVE
PO BOX 1867
BUFFALO NY 14240-9952

NO POSTAGE
NECESSARY
IF MAILED
IN THE
UNITED STATES

'You are welcome in my house,' he said firmly, 'but I didn't send for a doctor.'

'No, and you didn't come to my surgery, either, which was very remiss of you.'

'But I'm not ill.'

She slapped him on the back. 'And I aim to keep you that way,' she said with a heartiness calculated to terrorise any man. 'There's a flu epidemic in Palermo and I'm conducting a vaccination program to stop it reaching up here.'

'Flu,' he said dismissively.

'Don't sneer, it shows how little you know. Flu can be a killer, especially among the old. They're the ones who need to be vaccinated but they're resisting it because they still do things the old ways. So you'll have to give them a lead.'

'What?'

'You're the Great Man around here. If you lead they'll follow. You see, the trouble is, a lot of people are afraid of needles. Big strong men, some of them, and they can't face a little pinprick.'

'That will be all, Stella,' Bernardo said hastily. 'You can go now.'

When Stella had left Angie said, 'Very wise.' Her eyes were teasing.

He ground his teeth. 'Angie—'

'I think you should address me as *dottore*. It's more respectful.'

'Respectful!'

'Well, I think you ought to show me some respect,' she complained with a wounded look. 'Everybody else does. After all, the doctor is a pillar of the community.'

Goaded, he retorted, 'If you're such a pillar of the community, I don't think you ought to go around discussing your underwear in public.'

'Only for professional reasons. I'm setting my patients an example of how to combat the cold. And I have to demonstrate or there's no point.'

'You *show* people your underwear?' he demanded, aghast.

'Don't be stuffy. It's not as though I'm showing off black satin lingerie. There's nothing provocative about flannel "coms". Look.'

She pulled open her shirt to reveal the uncompromising red flannel underneath. Bernardo drew a sharp breath, hoping she wouldn't hear and guess that the electric jolt that had gone through his loins. Such prosaic underwear, but it filled him with thoughts and sensations that had nothing to do with red flannel.

Angie looked up at him, her eyes full of innocent fun. She knew he found her hard to cope with like this. It wasn't that Bernardo was humourless. He did have a sense of humour—lurking somewhere. But he lacked the flexible mind that could combine fun and serious purpose, as Angie was doing now.

'What are you up to?' he asked at last, and he sounded uneasy.

'Up to? I'm up to saving lives. I'm surprised you're so reluctant to help. You're protective about these people but you won't do this one little thing to help them.'

'All right, all right,' he said impatiently. 'I suppose you've come prepared. Do it, and then—please leave.'

But she shook her head. 'Not here and now. I want you to come to my surgery tomorrow morning. Be there at about eleven, that's when it's most crowded, and people will see you. Then the news will spread. I'll leave you in the waiting room for a few minutes, so that you can make sure everyone knows why you're there.'

He ground his teeth. 'Anything else?'

'Not tonight.'

'Then will you please leave?' he said tensely.

'You'll be there tomorrow?'

'I'll be there. Goodnight—*dottore*.'

She had half expected him to snub her next day but Bernardo was a man of his word, and he was there on the dot of eleven. When she glanced into the waiting room he was deep in conversation with a mother, with two children, and she overheard enough to know that he was doing as she'd asked. When it was his turn he waved ahead someone who had come in after him. Only when there was nobody left did he enter the surgery.

'Thank you, *signore*,' she said formally. 'I appreciate your help.'

She tried to keep her thoughts professional, but it was hard when the sight of him was so dear. When he pulled off his jacket and rolled up the sleeve of his dark red shirt she suddenly realised how much thinner he'd become since they'd quarrelled at the wedding. It hadn't struck her before, but as she held his arm she could feel that its strength was all sinew and nerves. Involuntarily she glanced up and met his eyes, then wished she hadn't. He was watching her with an unexpected gentleness that recalled the old days, and she couldn't afford to think of that just now. She still had too big a mountain to climb.

'You'll hardly feel it,' she said mechanically.

'Do you think a little needle-prick is the worst pain in the world?' he asked, quietly.

'Well, I suppose everyone has their own idea of the worst pain in the world,' she murmured. 'One person might be wounded to the heart by something another would ignore.'

'And one might understand pain so little that they thought they could play games.'

'If that's meant for me, it'll miss. I'm here to give these people a level of medical care they've never had before, and I'm not playing games.' She withdrew the needle and rubbed the spot with alcohol.

'Is that all you're here for?'

'I can't think of anything else, can you?' she asked, meeting his gaze.

'Not a thing.'

As she ushered him out they found a man in the waiting room, whom Angie had never seen before. He looked elderly, with lined, weather-beaten skin, and he was in a state of great agitation. He began to speak as soon as she appeared, gabbling in Sicilian that she found hard to follow, and falling over himself to get the words out. Bernardo put his hand on the man's shoulder and he began to calm down, although he still spoke urgently.

'What's the matter?' Angie asked Bernardo.

'His name is Antonio Servante,' Bernardo explained. 'He has a tiny farm a few miles from here which he farms alone except for his mother.'

'His *mother*? How old is he?'

'Sixty-five. He had a wife once, and two children, but they all died years ago in a measles epidemic.' Antonio seemed to be pleading for something. 'He wants you to vaccinate his mother,' Bernardo explained, 'but she's bedridden and he can't get her down here. His only transport is a mule. He says his mother is all he has in the world and he wants you to keep her alive.'

'Then I'll go to her, of course,' Angie said at once. Calling on her basic Sicilian, she told Antonio she would accompany him at once and he gave her a beaming, toothless smile.

'How are you going to travel?' Bernardo demanded. 'On his mule?'

'I've got a car.'

'I've seen it. It's pathetic. It'll never get you over that ground.'

'It's hired. I haven't had a chance to buy a proper one yet.'

'So how will you get to this place? And, when you get there, how will you communicate?'

She faced him. 'You tell me.'

'I warned you of something like this.'

'If you're going to say ''I told you so''—don't. Just—don't.'

'Wait here,' he said through gritted teeth. 'I'll get my car.'

Antonio, on his mule, led them down the road from Montedoro, then aside onto a winding road that climbed again and came out onto a flat stretch of earth that was the most barren and ugly she'd ever seen. There were stones everywhere, and she pitied anyone trying to scratch a living from this inhospitable place.

'I wonder how many of my patients are up here,' she murmured.

'Let's put it this way,' Bernardo said curtly, 'if they haven't got you, they haven't got anyone.'

'I haven't had time to go right through Dr Fortuno's lists. I'll have to do that soon.'

'I don't think he found his way up here very often, certainly not in winter. His old banger couldn't manage it, and you wouldn't catch him on a mule.'

'The sooner I get that car, the better.'

'You need one like mine, heavy-duty, four-wheel drive. Even so, it isn't going to take us all the way there. I've just remembered something.'

What he'd just remembered became evident in a few minutes. A steep hill reared up ahead of them, only negotiable by a path too narrow for a car. Dismayed, Angie got out and stared up the path to where Antonio was pointing.

'Is that it?' Angie asked, 'that house I can see?'

'That's the farmhouse, such as it is,' Bernardo agreed.

'Fine,' she said, speaking more cheerfully than she felt. 'Then we don't have very far to go.'

Antonio shyly took her arm and indicated for her to get onto the mule.

'I don't think—' she began hesitantly.

'It's the greatest honour he knows how to bestow,' Bernardo said. 'He loves Nesta almost as much as he loves his mother.' He added, 'and in mule terms she's almost as old.'

'Thanks,' Angie snapped.

He ground his teeth. 'Well, you wouldn't be told, would you?'

'Are you going to be useful?' she ground back. 'Or are you going to stand there gloating?'

'I am not gloating.'

'Well, you're certainly not being useful!'

Conscious of Antonio's eyes flicking from one to the other, Bernardo said in a tight voice, 'I'm going to carry your bag, so you'll have both hands free for holding on. You'll need them.'

She let Antonio help her onto Nesta's back, certain that the old animal was too small and frail for the burden. But Nesta stepped out confidently and began the journey up the steep incline. The path was about four feet wide, so that Angie could avoid looking down for most of the time. But suddenly they came upon a sharp turn which left her gazing down a long drop straight into the valley. She closed her eyes and the moment passed, but her head had swum sickeningly. She was never at ease with heights, yet she'd chosen a life where heights would be encountered daily. She wondered if there was any insanity in her family, or whether she was the first.

Antonio was walking at Nesta's head, encouraging her. Bernardo came up beside Angie, on the outside. 'Are you all right?' he asked quietly.

'I'm fine,' she said untruthfully. 'I wish you wouldn't walk there, so close to the edge.'

'I thought you might feel safer if I was between you and the drop.'

'That's nice, but honestly it just makes me worry about you. Anyway, you've got it quite wrong. I'm not afraid of heights.'

'I thought you were. That day in my home—'

'No, no,' she managed a laugh that came out sounding bright and confident, she couldn't think why. 'I was just taken by surprise that time.'

There was no need for him to answer because mercifully they had reached the top and were making their way to the tiny farm house. Angie saw that it was little more than a hovel, and she began to understand the kind of poverty she was dealing with.

Cecilia Servante came as a surprise. She was in her eighties but looked older, a little weatherbeaten gnome of a woman. But her eyes were bright and her voice lively. She couldn't get out of bed but she could backchat her son and send him scurrying into the kitchen to make coffee for their honoured guest. Angie was enchanted by her.

She spoke nothing but Sicilian. Taking a chance, Angie waved aside Bernardo's offer of help and tried to converse in her own tentative Sicilian. It turned out to be a smart move. Cecilia roared with laughter at her mistakes and spoke slowly to help her. In a few minutes Angie had learned some new phrases and established an excellent understanding with the old woman.

Her grip on life was still vigorous and to Angie's delight she was eager for the vaccination, pushing up her sleeve impatiently, then pointing to her son, cackling with laughter when he was squeamish at the needle.

Looking around her, Angie was horrified. Everywhere needed repair, everything was of the most basic. Antonio brought coffee and bread, which she guessed was a strain on his budget, but the law of hospitality was unbreakable. Her worst moment came when he reached into his pocket and brought out some money. It was a tiny amount, little more than one pound, but it was clear he could ill afford it. Then her quick wits came to her rescue.

'No money,' she said, holding up her hand as if to ward it off, and speaking slowly in Sicilian. 'Instead, you can do something for me. This room—Friday morning—I hold a clinic here. And you tell all your neighbours to be here. Yes?'

A smile broke over Antonio's face and he nodded vigorously, shoving the money back into his pocket with relief. He did his best to reply to her, but had to fall back on Bernardo.

'He says let him know what time, and he'll be waiting at the foot of the path with Nesta,' Bernardo translated.

They arranged the time, and Angie prepared to leave, with the sense that she had achieved something. But her smile died when she saw how fast the light had faded, leaving the path barely visible.

'Stay here while I go down to the car and get the torch,' Bernardo commanded.

'No way,' she said cheerfully. 'If I keep hold of the wall I'll be fine.'

'Will you please do as you're told?' he yelled.

'Nope. Let's get going.'

She set off briskly but he darted in front of her and hurried ahead. By the time she was half way down he was back with the torch, which he directed onto the path ahead of her. By this time it was completely dark and she was glad of the help, although she would have died sooner than admit it.

'Are you happy now?' Bernardo demanded savagely.

'Perfectly, thank you.'

'You won't do anything the sensible way, will you? Oh, no, that's too easy.'

'Well, it would have been easy if you'd remembered to take the torch from the car when we went up.'

'I didn't know you were going to be that long. How long does an injection take?'

'Ten seconds. But assessing my patient's general conditions takes a lot longer. You think a flu jab is all they need?'

'You can't give them all they need.'

'No, but I can give them a lot that nobody's ever bothered to give them before. Don't lecture me, Bernardo. You know nothing about it.'

'*I*—know nothing about it?'

'You were as horrified by that place as I was.'

'I could show you a hundred places like it. Are you going to single-handedly cure every ill in this place?'

'I'm going to try,' she said firmly. 'With or without your help. You talk about "your people" but what your people need is money. Filthy lucre. Spondulicks. Ill-gotten gains. All of which I have. If you really cared about them you'd have married me for my money and spent it all on them. Now, can we get back, please? I have evening surgery to do.'

CHAPTER SEVEN

FROM this beginning other good things flowed. On the Friday morning Antonio was waiting for her, as promised, with Nesta, and as she approached the farm house she saw the crowd gathered outside. He had spread the word enthusiastically.

Holding a local clinic had been an inspired idea. Many of her patients lived lives so isolated that coming into town was hard for them, even Montedoro in the low season. She hired Nesta and, as January passed into February, she began to go among them, sometimes travelling considerable distances, and improving her Sicilian all the time.

Bernardo tore his hair at these trips, but she refused his attempts to accompany her. She now had her own heavy-duty car, and pride made her do as much as possible without his help. Besides which, she wasn't short of assistance. Mayor Donati, determined to be seen 'taking a lead', was permanently at her disposal, plus there was a standing offer of help from Father Marco who had been her fan since discovering that she'd once tended a famous boxer for a minor injury.

Having investigated Dr Fortuno's not very well-kept lists, she went onto the offensive, travelling the district, meeting her patients, taking blood samples which she then sent off to the laboratory in Palermo. In this way she achieved one of her most dramatic early triumphs, demonstrating that Salvatore Vitello's violent thirst, which had made him the most notorious drunk in the area, was actually caused by diabetes.

His wife was in tears of relief but Vitello himself was sulkily ungrateful. His one claim to fame had been stripped from him. Instead of the admiration of young men as he quaffed the night away, his life was now governed by a diet sheet and pills, with the threat of daily injections if he didn't behave himself. When he met the *dottore* on the street he would, with his wife's eyes on him, bow and greet her with respect. But virtue had gone out of him, and he was a sadder, if healthier, man.

When Angie rose in the mornings there was an increasing sense of satisfaction that she was really achieving something. There was pleasure too in the way Ginetta was asking her questions—about how hard was it for a woman to become a doctor? And if she returned to school and studied, perhaps—? Angie trod a fine line between gently encouraging her and giving her unrealistic dreams. But Ginetta's grandmother, the woman she'd first met in the convent infirmary, was beginning to give her strange looks that had nothing to do with her trousers.

One morning something happened that really had nothing to do with anything. You had to see it in the right light to understand it. Pushing open her window and looking out onto the valley she saw a huge bird wheeling and circling, close enough for her to see that it was a golden eagle.

Angie held her breath as the beautiful creature swooped with the early morning sun on its huge wings, knowing she'd been given the sign of hope she longed for.

'I am an eagle,' she murmured to the unseen presence that was always in her heart. 'You'll see.'

It didn't all go smoothly. Nico Sartone, the local chemist, was Angie's enemy from the first day. In youth he'd

dreamed of being a doctor but lack of money had forced
him to abandon his studies. He was a competent chemist
and might have done much good, but he had delusions of
medical grandeur that had flowered unchecked during Dr
Fortuno's time. Patients with a well-founded distrust of
the old doctor had turned to Sortone for advice. Over the
years his business had flourished and so had his ego. Dr
Wendham, bright, young and brilliantly qualified, put his
nose severely out of joint.

Like any small community Montedoro had a good deal
of intermarriage, and the Sortone family tentacles
stretched far. There was soon a faction that didn't bother
to hide its disapproval of Angie, her foreign tongue, her
trousers, her insistence on living alone, her 'new-fangled'
ideas. But she fought back with medical care that even
Sortone couldn't fault, and some of his adherents wa-
vered. When he learned that his own sister-in-law had
brought her children to Angie for vaccination the result
was a sulphurous family row that reverberated through the
whole town. Thereafter Sortone was more careful, his attitude to her one of exaggerated respect, but she had no
illusions about his true feelings.

She experienced practical difficulties too. Once, while
she was out making visits on the mule, she got lost on
the way home, wandered for hours in the darkness and
was found by Antonio who'd called out a search party.
By that time she was drenched from a thunderstorm and
was laid low for three days with a heavy cold. But the
incident helped to consolidate her growing reputation.
Bernardo didn't come to call, but Stella visited every day,
bearing gifts.

'He told me to bring you this,' she said on the first day,
producing a bottle of wine. 'It's the best in his cellar.' In

a voice that mingled awe and admiration she added, 'He's very, very angry with you.'

'Tell him thank you,' Angie snuffled miserably.

'I will, when he telephones tonight.'

'Isn't he here?'

'No, he's spending a few days in Palermo, helping with preparations for Signora Martelli's birthday. But he'll call me to ask how you are.'

'He probably won't bother,' Angie said gloomily.

'He'll bother,' Stella said knowingly, and departed, leaving Angie to indulge in a coughing fit.

He could call *me*, she thought crossly. He won't, but he could.

He won't, though.

Even though he could.

But he won't.

And he didn't.

There were other gifts, a cake from the nuns, freshly baked bread from Father Marco's housekeeper, a ginger cake from Mayor Donati's wife, and enough bottles of wine to stock a tavern, much of it home-made. By most of the region she had been accepted.

She'd known about Baptista's birthday. Always a big event, this year it would mean more than ever, as Renato's wife was now part of the family. Heather had visited Angie once, and they had talked several times on the telephone, but much of her time was now taken up working for the Martelli firm, a fruit and vegetable wholesaler. She made several working trips abroad, and Britain was now considered 'her' terrain.

'Won't that put Lorenzo's nose out of joint?' Angie asked as the two of them sat cosily in her front room. 'It's always been his territory.'

Heather chuckled wickedly. 'Lorenzo doesn't want to

go back to London—not for a while, anyway. On his last trip he spent the night in a police cell.'

'For heaven's sake! Why?'

'He was arrested for driving over the limit. Plus he took a swipe at a policeman. I had to make a "mercy dash" over there to get him out. He's very happy to leave Britain to me in future.'

Thanks to Angie's precautions Montedoro had only three flu cases, who all recovered, but as soon as she was back to work two children went down with measles. Luckily they were both in the town, making visiting easy. She soon had the relief of knowing that the worst was probably over for both of them, but she continued to call twice a day, and as the date of the big party drew near she knew her chances of being there were slim.

Down below, Palermo was enjoying a typical mild Sicilian winter, albeit a rainy one. But up here in the mountains the weather was fast getting worse. Once it had been merely cold. Now the sky threatened snow. Reluctantly she called Baptista and explained that she dared not leave.

'Of course your patients come first, my dear,' said the old woman immediately. 'When the weather improves, you must come down and we'll have a long lunch together.'

Bernardo had returned from Palermo and paid her a brief call to enquire after her health. He remained for only a short time, as if this was a duty he wanted to get over quickly, but he did offer to take her to Palermo for the party, 'since I know you dislike driving over mountain roads.'

She'd accepted the offer, and enjoyed a few fantasies about the time they would spend together, the brilliantly lit Residenza, the music, the dancing, the journey home, warmed by the glow of the previous evening…

But on the morning of the party, when Bernardo called to collect her, he found her waiting for him despondently.

'I can't go,' she said. 'Can you take my gift to Baptista for me?'

'But it's her birthday. She's only happy if she has everyone around her.'

'I daren't leave Montedoro. There have already been a few flakes of snow. Suppose the weather closes in and I can't get back for days? What are the people here supposed to do for a doctor? I've talked to Baptista, and she agrees with me. But you should go quickly.'

'This is madness. Dr Fortuno took a few days off whenever he wanted.'

'Well, I doubt anyone noticed the difference,' Angie said wryly. 'He may have been a dear old man, but he was a rotten doctor. He left me all his books and medical journals, and I found nothing less than thirty years old. I'd love to know what sort of qualifications he had. A certificate in First Aid, probably. And I'll bet the only reason he was here was that nobody else wanted the job.'

'My father helped him get it,' Bernardo said. 'I recall him saying that Fortuno hadn't exactly passed top of the class.'

'So why didn't you get your people a proper doctor?'

'Because I didn't know what you've just told me. Not passing well didn't mean he was no good for a practice where not much happens.'

'But why didn't things happen? Because they gave up on him. My waiting room is full every day with people who never bothered to come before, because they knew there was no point.'

'And how would I have got anyone else?' he demanded. 'You said yourself, people aren't falling over themselves to work here.'

'You should have gone out and found someone. There are loads of bright, starry-eyed young doctors who wouldn't mind starting here if someone gave them financial help. You could have offered that. Anyway, they've got me now, and I'm going to be here when they need me.'

'Does that mean you can never enjoy yourself?'

She shrugged. 'You warned me that it would be tough.'

At the doorway he paused. 'What happens when you get fed up and decide to leave for good? What do they do then?'

'Maybe I won't leave.'

'You will—in the end. And how can anyone afford to buy this place with all the new equipment you've put in?'

'They probably couldn't. So I'll have to stay. Now get going. And give my love to Baptista.'

That night it began to snow. Angie watched the white flakes through her bedroom window, and realised that by morning the road up here would be impassable. She had done the right thing in remaining. She tried to make herself feel better with that thought, but it was hard when the wind was howling around the little village in its exposed position.

And of course, her good intentions would all be wasted. Nobody would fall ill. Nothing would happen. She would spend several days snowed in alone, when she could have been in Palermo enjoying a convivial time at the Residenza.

If only the wind would die down, she thought, moving restlessly about the room. She ought to go to bed, but she knew she wouldn't sleep in the centre of this turbulence.

It took her an hour, but at last she dozed off and awoke

to an eerie silence. For once there was no sound from the street outside. Making her way to the window that over-looked the valley, she found herself gazing out onto a scene from another world.

Snow stretched as far down as she could see, which wasn't very far. Then it vanished into a thick mist. The mist had crept up during the night, cutting off the moun-tain peak from the valley below, so that it was as though Montedoro floated above the clouds. In one sense it was magical. In another it was desolating. This was what Bernardo had warned her about, but he'd never told her that he would leave her to face it alone. For the first time she began to understand the distance he was determined to set between them, and her heart almost failed her. The tide of hope and optimism that had carried her here began to look like foolishness: a spoilt young woman's convic-tion that what she wanted was hers for the asking.

She got up and made herself breakfast. She would be alone today as she'd given Ginetta some time off. She made sure everything was ready in the surgery but when she looked out there was only an empty street, and un-trodden snow in both directions.

She logged onto the net and spent most of the day ac-cessing medical journals and chasing the latest news.

'Stay up to date,' her father had said. 'If they discover it today, you learn about it tomorrow. Never fall behind. It's the quickest way to get brain-dead.'

She'd always found this part of her work fascinating, but now she knew she was working from the top of her head, reading but not taking in. She downloaded several articles for later when her brain was functioning.

In the early afternoon she made herself a snack and poured a glass of Bernardo's wine. Then she wished she hadn't. It looked forlorn, standing by her plate in solitary

festivity. The house was dreadfully quiet. When she
looked out the snow in the street showed not a single
footmark. Nobody had ventured out all day. They were
all safely shut up in their homes, and already, as the winter
light faded, she could see the windows start to glow.

A person could feel sorry for themselves in this situation, she reflected. She'd stayed here for their sakes, and
not one of them had the decency to develop so much as
a sore thumb.

She went around the house, drawing the curtains, trying
not to hear the lonely sound of her footsteps on the flagstones. At her bedroom window she pushed open the case-
ment for a last look down into the valley before darkness
fell completely. Then she stopped and peered, trying to
decide if she'd really spotted something or only imagined
it.

It was almost impossible to see, but she thought she
could discern a dark shadow emerging from the mist. She
wasn't mistaken. Somebody was down there, struggling
up the steep, snow-covered road to Montedoro. But who
would be mad enough to attempt that road on foot in this
weather?

She screwed up her eyes, trying to hold the stumbling
figure in view as the darkness grew more impenetrable,
until he vanished altogether.

'He hasn't even got a torch,' she muttered. 'Idiot!'

But at least it meant there was someone who needed
her, which was almost a relief. Pulling on some trousers,
her thick boots and a coat, she seized up a heavy duty
torch and went out into the street.

It was hard to keep her balance on the steep slope and
she had to move at a snail's pace, keeping hold of the
wall until at last she reached the huge stone gate that
marked the entrance to the town. She swung her torch in

an arc down the mountain road, but there was no sign of anyone. She began to inch her way down, waving the beam and calling, although in the high wind she couldn't be sure that her voice was carrying. She could hear nothing back, and she wondered if the traveller had collapsed.

Her alarm grew as she went further and further down, frantically straining her eyes and calling out. At last she saw him, sitting by the side of the road, his arms resting on his knees. He looked up just as she scrambled down beside him.

'Are you hurt?' she gasped, looking into his face. *'Bernardo!'*

He was equally astonished. 'What are you doing here?' he mumbled through lips that were almost numb with cold.

'I saw you from my window. What do you mean walking up here without even a torch? Where's your car?'

'I had to leave it further down the road. It wasn't safe to drive in that mist. I have a torch but the batteries failed.' He was talking in a series of gasps as though his lungs were protesting after the long haul upwards.

'Are you hurt?' she demanded.

'I turned my ankle some way back.'

'Put your arm around my shoulder.'

'I can manage without—'

'Just do it,' she interrupted him firmly. 'I've got to get you home before you freeze to death.'

He grimaced but obeyed her. Clutching the low wall with one hand and her with the other, he managed to get upright and they began the slow journey up the rest of the way to Montedoro. Angie's mind was full of questions. How far had he come on foot? And why was he here at all? But there would be time to think of that later. She could feel that he was at the end of his strength.

At last, to her vast relief, her door came in sight. But as she went to open it Bernardo said, 'I'll go to my own house.'

'You'll do as your doctor tells you,' she said crossly. 'I need to look at that ankle, and I prefer to do it in my surgery.'

He didn't try to argue any further.

In fact, she didn't take him into the surgery, but into her front room. After helping him off with his coat she pushed him gently down onto the sofa and went into the kitchen, returning a moment later with a tumbler half full of a golden brown liquid.

'Brandy,' she said. 'Thaw you out. Heaven knows, you need it.'

While he drained the glass she went to find a thick, towelling robe that she'd purposely bought four sizes too large because she enjoyed snuggling into it.

'Your clothes are sodden right through,' she told him. 'Take everything off and put this on. Go on, I won't look. I'll be getting you some more brandy.'

When she returned he was wearing the robe and she got to work on his foot, exclaiming as she touched his freezing flesh. 'How long had you been walking?'

'I don't know. Hours.'

To her relief the ankle was neither broken nor sprained, but merely wrenched, although it was suffering from the burden he'd put on it.

'How soon did you do this?' she asked, testing the swelling.

'Almost at once.'

'You haven't done it any good walking on it. What possessed you? Why didn't you turn back, use your mobile to call someone to drive up and collect you?'

'I wanted to reach Montedoro,' he said irritably. 'It

seemed a good idea then but now I'm not sure why. Quit nagging!'

'Your face is bruised and your head cut,' she said. 'How did that happen?'

'When I fell I was on a very steep part of the road, and it was icy. I slipped back several feet.' He showed her his hands, lacerated where he'd tried to grip the cobbles.

Alarmed, she checked him all over, but found to her relief that there were no broken or cracked bones. She bathed his cuts and put some sticking plaster on his head. By now he was leaning back with his eyes closed, as though the sudden warmth, lack of food and two hefty slugs of brandy had caught up with him all in a moment.

Quietly Angie went into the kitchen and began to prepare some food. As she worked she continually glanced up at the sight of him, out like a light. She felt happier than she'd been for a long time. He might say what he liked, but he'd returned because she was here, and he wouldn't leave her alone. When the going got tough, he ought to have turned back. But he hadn't.

He jumped when she touched him on the shoulder. 'Hot soup,' she said.

He rubbed his eyes. 'I should go home.'

'Soup,' she said inexorably, handing him the bowl and the spoon.

When she saw him eating she fetched her own soup and sat down facing him over the low table. After the soup came something hot and filling that she'd micro-waved straight from the freezer. It wasn't exactly cuisine, but he ate as though he was too tired to know what he was doing.

Just as he finished eating the telephone in the kitchen rang. It was Baptista, sounding concerned.

'Do you know if Bernardo got home safely?' she asked.

'He would insist on leaving just when the weather was closing in.'

'He's here,' Angie said. 'He arrived an hour ago.'

'An hour? But he left this morning.'

'He had to do the last part on foot.'

'Then he is lucky to be alive. There was no talking him out of it. I'll stop worrying now. I know he's safe with you. Goodbye, my dear. May this year be a happy one for you.'

'Goodbye Baptista. And—thank you.'

She was smiling to herself as she replaced the receiver and returned to Bernardo. He was lying full length on the sofa, dead to the world. Quietly she removed the dishes and draped a blanket over him.

She went to bed but left the door open between the bedroom and the main room. In the thick blackness she couldn't see him, but she could just make out the sound of his breathing. She lay listening until she fell asleep.

She awoke with a start. The dark was still impenetrable but she could hear the sound of someone stumbling around, muttering. Quickly she slipped out of bed and made her way towards the noises. She was about to put on a light when an arm came out of nowhere, curling about her neck, and the next moment she was holding most of Bernardo's weight, slumped against her. Instinctively she closed her arms about him.

'What are you doing in my house?' he muttered. 'Oh, lord, my head!'

'Probably all that brandy,' she said softly.

'I never drink brandy.'

'You did last night. You needed it.'

'I need my bed. I can't find the bedroom.'

'Come with me,' she whispered. 'I'll take you.'

Inch by inch she moved back towards the bedroom. He

came with her unresisting, only half awake, seeming now to accept her presence as normal. She supported him as far as her bed, then let him fall gently on it, and drew her thick duvet over him. He was deeply asleep in a moment.

The duvet was huge, to match the bed, and there was room for her to slip beneath it without touching him. She longed to put her arms about him, but she didn't dare yield to the temptation. They had a long way to go yet.

But her heart sang because she knew he had come back for her.

She was awoken by the feel of an unaccustomed weight on her breast. Opening her eyes she saw that it was Bernardo's head, which had found its place by instinct. He was holding her tightly with one arm thrown over her as though he found in her something that he needed.

She realised that he was no longer wearing the robe. He'd had it on when he came to bed, so she guessed his movements must have dislodged it.

Very, very gently she dared to touch his hair, and felt it springy against her fingers. At once she snatched her hand away, fearful of waking him. But the next moment she reached out again, relishing the pleasure of touching him.

She had missed him so much. It had been bad enough during the long weeks in England but since she'd returned to Sicily, living within a stone's throw of him, the ache of longing had been worse.

On the surface things were going well. Despite his warnings she'd been a big success with her patients. There were still some prejudices to overcome but they weren't fools. They knew they stood to benefit from her up-to-date equipment and even more up-to-date attitude, and they had given her a chance. Even Bernardo had been forced to accord her respect.

Plus there was the satisfaction of knowing that she'd surprised him. She'd challenged him, laughed at him, turned all his expectations on their heads. He no longer knew how to cope with her, and serve him right!

But in the essentials nothing had changed. Behind the civility, even the occasional smile, they were almost as far apart as ever. And there was the added torment of seeing him every day, wondering about his thoughts and feelings.

For she could overcome his doubts about her commitment, but the true barrier was something more elusive. If he had been merely too proud to take money from a woman, that she could have understood. But his revulsion at her wealth came from a darkness deep inside the man that she couldn't confront because he wouldn't let her.

So now she would make the most of the few precious minutes when he was hers, for she didn't know how long they would last. His skin felt so good beneath her hands, and his head so right nestling against her. He stirred and burrowed more closely, and she risked tangling her fingers in his hair.

She felt the first movement of his lips against the swell of one breast and drew a long breath. She must stop this now, quickly, before he awoke. But—just one more moment—and one more—

The sound of his voice reached her so faintly that she had to strain to listen. He'd murmured something—her name? After holding her breath for a long time she realised that the moment had passed, and she would never know.

This was how it should have been. This was the life they should have had, being together, loving in peace, facing their problems as a team instead of being driven apart by shadows that couldn't be fought.

She set her chin. There must be no talking like that. Anything could be fought, and she was here to fight it. He was hers and she wouldn't let him go.

He whispered something again and she felt the heat of his breath against her skin.

'Yes, my dear,' she murmured, enveloping him in strong, protective arms. 'We're going to win, do you hear? Whatever I have to do, we're going to win.'

CHAPTER EIGHT

AT LAST Bernardo slackened his grip and she could ease herself carefully from under him. He didn't awake, and she managed to slip from the bed and pull on a light robe before going into the kitchen.

The light startled her. In the bedroom the wooden shutters were drawn across the windows, blocking out the light. Now she realised that they had both slept very late and it was nearly ten o'clock in the morning. Luckily it was Sunday, Ginetta's day off, and they wouldn't be disturbed. She was smiling as she began to make the coffee.

The soft rustle of her movements as she left the bed was enough to awaken Bernardo. At first he lay very still, baffled by the unfamiliar surroundings. This was neither his room nor his bed. Nor did he feel very much like himself. The man he knew himself to be had gone to sleep in the snow and darkness a thousand years ago. He didn't know how he'd been transported to this place so that he awoke bathed in warmth and well-being. He only knew that he wanted to stay here forever.

As more of his surroundings came into focus he became aware that the far side of the bed was warm and sweet-smelling. There was a dent, too, in the other pillow. Inspecting it more closely he found a single hair. It was blonde, fluffy and intensely feminine.

Then it all came back to him, the driving need to return to this place to watch over her, the journey that had turned into a nightmare, and the presence that had materialised out of the darkness to take him home. She'd tended him,

122

fed him, then left him asleep on her sofa. He remembered that bit very clearly now.

What he couldn't recall was how he'd come to be sleeping in her bed.

Naked.

Or what he'd done once he was there.

He tried frantically to kick start his memory, but it was hard when it was so entwined with his longings. In his dreams he'd made love with her so often that it was impossible now to be sure whether the pictures in his mind were memories or imagination.

He sat up, shaking his head. The movement caused the robe to slide right off the bed. He made a grab for it, missed, and was about to lean out for it when the sound of Angie's footsteps made him hastily retreat under the duvet.

She appeared with coffee, smiling when she saw him awake. He tried to read that smile, to guess what she expected of him. But though friendly, her eyes gave nothing away.

'Have you rejoined the human race?' she asked.

What did that mean?

'I've thawed out,' he said carefully.

'Good. There was a time I thought that would never happen. Which side do you want your coffee?'

'Pardon?'

'You're in the middle of the bed. Do you want to lean over here or that side?'

'Over here is fine,' he said, indicating the side where she was standing, and inching his way over. She sat on the bed and he clutched the duvet.

'You were like an icicle, when I found you on the road,' she observed, setting down the coffee.

'Pretty near a dead icicle,' he admitted. 'Thank you, *dottore*.'

'*Dottore?*' she asked, looking amused.

What, in heaven's name, had he called her last night? He had an unnerving feeling it hadn't been *dottore*.

'I never thought to hear you say thank you,' she said with a shake of the head that made her soft hair dance wickedly about her cheeks. She smiled, meeting his eyes significantly, and he drew the duvet a little more firmly around him. 'You just never know what's going to happen next, do you?'

'No,' he agreed, not taking his eyes from her. 'Life is full of surprises.'

'And some things are more of a surprise than others.'

That reply was like a blow over the solar plexus. It was true, then. She really had lain in his arms, offering him all herself, whispering his name in her delight, asking everything, giving everything...

And he couldn't even remember it properly.

Angie was trying to collect her scattered wits. Her eyes would insist on fixing themselves on his bare chest. She could still feel where his arm had been flung over her, where his head had lain against her and his breath had warmed her. If only she knew whether he'd been aware of that. Had he known when he moved his lips against her and murmured words she couldn't hear? Did he remember it now? Did he regret it? What 'surprises' was he thinking of?

She searched his eyes. They gave nothing away.

'If you'll go away for a moment,' he said, 'I'll get up.'

'Oh, no, you don't. You're staying in that bed. You nearly froze to death yesterday and I'm going to take care of you. That's what a doctor is for.'

He frowned. 'Did I get a bang on the head?'

'Not that I know of. Why?'

'There are gaps in my memory. I'm sure I went to sleep on your sofa.'

How did I get into your bed? At what point, exactly, did I discard my clothes?

'I found you wandering around in the night. You were half asleep and confused. You thought you were back in your own home. I thought you'd be more comfortable in here.'

'Is—that all?'

'That's all.'

Perhaps he'd imagined her little sigh of regret. Or perhaps he'd only heard it inside himself.

'It's time I made you something to eat,' she said. 'English breakfast, bacon, eggs, sausage, tomato, fried bread. And you'll have it in bed.'

By the time she returned with a laden tray he'd retrieved the robe from the floor, tucked it decently around him and was back under the duvet. He'd meant to stride out determinedly and insist on sitting at the table, with dignity. But suddenly it was pleasant to be looked after, and he stayed where he was.

Besides, she looked so pretty with her face flushed from the stove, and her ridiculous hair wafting around it in tendrils. How could a doctor have hair like that?

'Bernardo,' she said patiently, trying to get through his glazed expression.

'What?' Startled, he came back to reality.

'I asked you to straighten your knees. I can't put the tray down.'

'Sorry.' He complied and they settled matters efficiently. 'Aren't you having anything?'

'Just getting it.'

She returned and sat on the bed, with a large mug in

her hands. It was a child's mug, covered in cartoon characters, and right this minute she looked little more than a child.

'Is that all?'

'This is English tea. It'll set me up for the day.'

'Is that what I've got?' he asked with misgiving.

'No, I made you coffee.'

'Let me try that.' He took a sip from her mug, made a face and nearly choked. 'Good grief!' he said, reaching hastily for his coffee, and they laughed together.

'How did the party go?' she asked.

'Wonderfully well,' he said, tucking in and speaking between mouthfuls. 'Renato has finally made up with Lorenzo. I mean *really* made up. Before we went down to the guests we had a drink together, and Renato toasted Lorenzo, saying he owed his happiness to him. He said they all knew Heather and Lorenzo's wedding was a mistake, and Lorenzo was the only one who had the nerve to do anything about it.'

'Which is true,' Angie mused.

'Yes, it is.' Bernardo gave an ironic grin. 'If Lorenzo hadn't been brave enough to be a coward, Heather and Renato wouldn't be as happy as they are today.'

'Are they really, do you think?'

'They're in love. They belong together but Renato screwed it all up by trying to marry her to Lorenzo.'

'Why did he do that, I wonder?'

'Because he was enjoying his life as it was, a string of girlfriends and no commitments. But someone had to marry and provide an heir so he cast Lorenzo as "the sacrificial lamb"—that's how Lorenzo puts it. But you should see Renato now, the very picture of the happily married man, *and*—' Bernardo paused, grinning.

'*No!*' Angie exclaimed. 'Is Heather—?'

'There's no announcement, but Baptista's certain. She says she can "tell".'

'That would be wonderful,' Angie said with a touch of wistfulness. 'A baby. They'll be a real family at last.'

'Nothing matters as much as family,' Bernardo agreed. 'That's why Baptista likes to have everyone around her on her birthday.'

'Tell me about the rest of the evening. Did she like my gift?'

'She loved it. The hall was filled with hothouse flowers that Heather had bought from some fellow who specialises in winter blooms. He was there, and he turned out to be an old friend of hers, from far back in her youth. Federico, I think his name was. She seemed very happy to see him.'

'I'm glad,' Angie said sincerely. 'I love Baptista.'

Bernardo paused, not looking at her. 'So do I,' he said after a moment. He looked at her. 'You should have been there.'

'If you knew how much I wanted to.' She chuckled ruefully. 'And nothing happened. Nobody so much as cut their thumb.'

'But you were right about the weather,' he admitted.

'Why did you try to get back, Bernardo?'

Silly question. The answer was there in his eyes, fixed on her.

'You'd think I'd have known better,' he said. 'But—I didn't.'

'Do you have to be wise all the time?' she asked wistfully.

'I'm not so very wise, Angie.'

He made a slight movement and the tray tilted, forcing him to grab it just in time. Angie took it hastily and removed everything to the safety of the kitchen.

He leaned back against the pillows in a state of deep

content. It was a strange feeling, and one he'd never
known before—or not for twenty years. After a good
night's sleep and a large breakfast he should be ready to
leap out of bed. Instead a heaviness seemed to weigh
down his limbs, and he wanted only to stay here, happy
to be in her hands. For years he'd known no comfort such
as this, nobody to say, 'Stay there and let me look after
you.' He hadn't asked for it, couldn't take it, and would
have fiercely rejected the offer.

But suddenly it was simple. All you had to do was give
in, let go, trust somebody you loved. Slowly he slid down
in the bed, abandoning himself to the sweet warmth and
content that he wanted to last for ever. It was bliss to be
free from strain, to let the thoughts fade away, taking the
worries with them.

Angie set things down quietly in the kitchen and went
quickly back to the bedroom, her heart singing. Their
troubles were over. She'd made the longed-for break
through, he would open his arms in welcome, and then...

She pushed open the bedroom door.

He was asleep.

But he couldn't be. He'd only just woken up.

Then her indignation faded as she crept closer and saw
that his face was as she'd never seen it before, relaxed
and untroubled, like a child's face before the discovery of
pain. He looked as if he might actually know how to be
happy, and that too was new, she realised.

Tenderness wrenched at her heart. She wanted to enfold
him in her arms and promise to make everything well for
him. Moving softly, she eased herself onto the bed and
dared to stroke his hair. He stirred but didn't awaken. He
looked, she realised, as though nothing could awaken him
for a long time, as though he were sleeping away the cares
of a whole lifetime.

And perhaps, she thought, that was what he needed to do. She crept away, closing the door softly behind her.

He lay almost motionless for the rest of the day and most of the evening. Sometimes Angie would look in, hear his even breathing, and back quietly out again. It might have seemed like a wasted day, but she was certain that in the peaceful silence his barriers were coming down. Her time would come.

Late in the evening, after a shower, she slipped into the bedroom, and quietly opened the shutters to look out on the mountains. The brilliant moon turned the snow to silver and cast a pale glow over the bedroom. The sudden light caused Bernardo to stir, and in an instant she was there beside him, reaching out, touching his face. Then his eyes opened directly on her, and there was a look in them that made her heart beat faster.

'Have you been there all the time?' he murmured.

She shook her head. 'Only the last few minutes.'

'I thought you were there—you seemed to be with me every moment.'

'Only my heart—*amor mio.*'

He opened his arms to her, and now she was free to go into them, returning his eager embrace with all her heart.

'Let me hold you,' he said thickly. 'I've thought about nothing else.'

His mouth cut off her answer. His hands were pulling away the towel, drawing her naked body against his own. She ran her hands luxuriously over him, savouring its hard, compact maleness, the steely, tensile strength. She wanted him so much she could hardly bear it.

It seemed as though he would kiss her everywhere at once. His lips dropped burning kisses on her mouth, her neck, her breasts. They were already full and peaked with desire for him, waiting for him to tease them lovingly.

She let out a long gasp of pleasure at the feel of his tongue rasping gently against first one, then the other, taking his time, letting the pleasure build slowly, taking her over, while she entwined her fingers in his hair and gave herself up to her feelings.

'You're so beautiful,' he murmured, regarding her in the moonlight. 'I've tried to picture you so often, but I never came close to the reality.'

'Not even in red flannel ''coms''?' she teased.

He gave a splutter of laughter. She joined in and then his arms were tight around her again, his head against her breast, laughing helplessly, and it was a good sound from this man who found it so hard to laugh.

'You wretch,' he growled. 'You were tormenting me that day on purpose.'

'Yes,' she said, 'and what are you going to do about it?'

'This,' he said, teasing her purposefully, 'and this—'

'Oh, darling—*yes*—'

She offered herself joyfully to his increasingly intimate caresses, telling him by her movements that she was his whenever he wished. But a fever of impatience was growing in her and she ached with the need to be one with him.

At last he moved over her, moving slowly, always waiting for her until he was certain that her desire was in harmony with his own. She reached up for him, eager to feel him inside her, and as he entered she gave a soft cry of need and fulfilment that was cut off by the pressure of his lips.

How could such perfect union be achieved at the first loving? Or perhaps it was a first loving in name only, and these two had already loved each other to satiety in their hearts and souls before their bodies were matched. Angie only knew each of her movements was informed by her deep knowledge of him, and that every touch, every caress he gave her was instinctively perfect.

In the moonlight she could see his face, not completely, but enough to discern its gentle expression. This man, so rough and awkward in his everyday life, had the subtlety to grow close to a woman when he didn't have to use words. And he had the tenderness to make her heart over-flow, as long as he could show his feelings in actions, in caresses, and soft murmurings.

He could read her wishes by instinct, and knew exactly the moment to hold back and give her time, then reclaim the initiative and love her more vigorously. And as she felt this she gave herself up to him joyfully, knowing that she could trust him at least as well as she could trust herself.

Afterwards as she nestled against him, she received an-other surprise. In all her earlier relationships—mini-loves, as she thought of them, not to be compared with this love that swamped all others—she had never been troubled by jealousy. She felt it now for the first time.

It was easy to guess how much competition there would be for Bernardo's attention, she thought. Behind him stretched a whole hinterland of thoughts, feelings, trou-bles—and loves—of which she knew nothing. And sud-denly it mattered.

'What are you thinking to make you so quiet?' he mur-mured.

'Thoughts you wouldn't like,' she said darkly. 'Posses-sive thoughts, jealous thoughts.'

He laughed, the first natural, trouble free amusement she'd ever heard from him.

'You're wrong,' he said. 'I do like that.'

'Oh, really?'

'It's nice to know all the possessiveness isn't on my side. But never be jealous, *amor mia*. Whatever has been in the past, now there is only you.'

'Whatever—has—been—in—the—past?' she echoed slowly.

'In future there is only you. Come here—and let me show you.'

CHAPTER NINE

ANGIE awoke at first light, still warm and luxuriously full of his loving. But when she stretched out her arms the bed was empty. Bernardo was sitting by the window looking down into the valley as it emerged silently from the grey mists. She slipped out of bed, pulled on a wrap and went to him. He didn't look at her, but his arms went about her at once, drawing her tightly against him.

'What are you looking at down there?' she whispered.

His reply surprised her. 'Ghosts.'

'Are there many?'

'Too many.'

'Your parents?'

'Yes, but not only them. There's one other who haunts and torments me—' He stopped and she felt the tremor go through him.

'Come back to bed, my love,' she said, although she knew it wasn't cold that had made him shiver. She wanted to get him away from that window and whatever troubling visions it revealed to him.

He let her lead him back to bed, and when they were under the covers they clung together. She held him with a kind of tender triumph, confident that she'd won him at last, and from now on the future would be what they made it together. His hold on her was different, for in him need was as great as love. She sensed that and made love to him with profound tenderness, trying to tell him that she could be all he needed.

Once she saw him regarding her face with a look almost

of desperation. She smiled to reassure him, and when he laid his head against her neck she wrapped her arms about him in a gesture of reassurance. She thought she felt him relax, and smiled to herself. It had been hard but she had found the way at last.

Afterwards she snuggled contentedly against him. He'd half pulled himself up against the bedhead and sat staring abstractedly into space. Once arm was about her, drawing her against his bare chest, but she sensed that he was engrossed in thoughts that shut her out. She was too deeply in love with him to accept that without protest.

'Hey,' she murmured gently.

He smiled quickly and she had the feeling that she'd brought him back from some polar region.

'What are you thinking?' she asked.

'Nothing much.'

'Is it nothing much that makes you frown like that? Tell me.'

When he didn't answer she asked, 'Are the ghosts there still?'

'They are always there.'

'Even now?'

'Now more than ever. They cry loudest when they tell me that I have no right to be happy.'

'But why should they say that?'

He didn't answer and suddenly she was frightened. She'd thought that all problems between them were solved, and now she found herself confronted with something she didn't understand, and that he wouldn't explain.

'Tell me,' she insisted.

'I can't.'

She fell back on the age-old plea. 'Then you don't love me. If you did you wouldn't shut me out.'

Suddenly the happy contentment she'd seen in him before vanished, and his face was distraught. 'Angie, don't do this, I beg you.'

'Why not? You've shut me out for so long and I'm tired of being shut out. How much do you think I can take? Tell me what's troubling you.'

Again she saw his look of desperation, as though the joy they had brought each other was only a mirage. Suddenly she couldn't cope. A moment ago she'd thought that she'd won, but now it was all slipping through her fingers and she didn't know why.

'Where were you these last few hours?' she demanded frantically. 'I thought we were making love—'

'We were—'

'No, you were somewhere else—with your ghosts.'

She felt him flinch. 'No woman has ever meant to me what you do. Let that be enough, for pity's sake!'

His refusal to open up to her was like a blow. She pulled away and stared at him, hostile and now as withdrawn as he.

'How can it be enough?' she asked at last, trying to speak calmly through the hurt. 'We make love, but I feel I'm nothing to you because you're hiding from me.'

He ran his hands distractedly through his hair. 'And what will be enough? When you've forced me to tell you things that I can't bear to look at myself? Will that be enough?'

'If I'm no use to you—'

'Use? I don't want you to be a doctor for me. I want you to love me.'

'I do love you—'

'Oh, yes, but it must be on your terms. You have to own a man's soul as well as his heart. I was right to be wary of you.'

Silence fell between them. It was an ugly, mistrustful silence and she felt as if she were dying inside.

'Don't look like that,' he begged.

'I don't know how I look,' she said wretchedly. 'I don't know what to say to you any more. I think perhaps what happened between us last night—shouldn't have happened.'

He paled. 'Do you really mean that?'

'I don't know.'

He took her face between his hands. 'Don't, my love,' he implored. 'Don't let a shadow fall between us. It's nothing—nothing—'

'How can it be nothing when it makes you look like that, and turn away from me? I don't think it's nothing. I think it's the thing that drives you. Don't ask me how I know that. I just do.'

'Then I think you must be a witch to know so much.'

'So much?' she echoed bitterly. 'I don't really know much, do I? You won't let me. You talk about love on my terms, but what about yours? You want to give just so much of yourself, and no more. That isn't love.'

'Darling—please—*please*—'

'Tell me,' she cried in anguish. 'Who is the third ghost?'

He sighed as though too weary to fight any longer. After a long moment he said, 'The third ghost is a boy of twelve, who lives alone with his mother. Sometimes his father visits them, but he isn't married to his mother, and he has another family at a big house by the sea. They are his legal family, they are acknowledged, they bear his name.

'The boy bears only his mother's name, and secretly he is ashamed. He is ashamed even of his shame, for she is a good mother and loves him. She tells him how scared she is of the legal wife who lives in the big house because she knows the wife hates her for taking the man's love.

'The boy tries to be everything she wants, but secretly he longs to visit the great house and see his father's family. And so one day he slips away and goes down the mountain alone. Nobody sees him, and nobody knows where he's gone. He's away many hours, but he doesn't reach his destination. It gets dark and there is too far to travel, so he turns back. When he gets home the house is dark. He goes in and waits for his mother to return, but the hours pass and she doesn't come home.

'Then somebody comes to the house to tell him that both his parents are dead. The father came to see his mother that day. They were worried by his absence and went out in the car to search for the boy. But the car turned over on the mountain, and they both died.'

'Oh, my God!' Angie whispered, but Bernardo didn't seem to hear her. He'd slipped away into the nightmare that he never really escaped.

'He never told anyone why he'd gone away,' he said, 'but in his heart he knew that he'd killed them. To his mother, especially, he'd been disloyal. And then a few days later the wife came to see him. She was the woman whose hatred his mother had feared, but she spoke to him kindly, and told him that he was to live in his father's house and bear his father's name, like his other sons.

'And so he gained everything he'd wanted—at the price of two lives. He should have told her honestly that he'd killed her husband. Then she would have turned against him and sent him away to an institution, where he belonged. But he couldn't bear to tell the truth. He was a coward, you see.'

'No,' she said urgently. 'He was a child.'

'He isn't a child now. He's kept silent all these years because by not speaking out then he made it impossible to speak out at all. And so he's met all her attempts at kindness with churlish suspicion, always wondering how much she secretly hates him—'

'That's not fair to Baptista,' Angie said quickly. 'She doesn't hate you.'

'Perhaps. But what would she say if she knew the truth?'

'I don't know. But I don't think she'd blame you—a child of twelve.'

'I didn't feel like a child. I felt like a man. Whenever he left us, my father would say, "Remember to care for your mother. That is a man's duty." But instead of caring for her I—' A shudder racked him. *'Dear God!'*

Her instinct had been right, she thought. This was the thing that drove him, but now he'd trusted her enough to reveal it they could cope with it together, and all would be well. She put her arms about his shaking body, holding him close in a passion of tenderness and love.

'It's all right, my darling,' she murmured. 'Hold onto me. I'm here. We can make everything right.'

'It'll never be right,' he groaned.

'It will, it will—if we love each other—'

As she spoke she was seducing him with her hands, touching and caressing him everywhere, trying to draw him back to her. Little by little she felt his physical resistance to her slacken, until he yielded, with a groan, to their mutual desire.

His lovemaking was different now, less tender, more driven, as though there was something that he desperately wanted from her. She gave him everything she had to give, revelling in his need of her. She felt strong and triumphant that night, and when she looked into his face, and saw its tenderness replaced by a look of haunting fear, it was easy to tell herself that she was mistaken.

*   *   *

She was awoken by the sound of Ginetta moving about in the kitchen. The room was filled with light and she guessed the sun must be high. It wasn't like her to over-sleep, but the night had been so full—she smiled at the memory—that she'd needed an extra sleep.

The other side of the bed was empty, and after the first disappointment she realised that Bernardo's sense of pro-priety had made him slip away before Ginetta could find him there.

Never mind, she thought happily. Soon they would be ready to tell the world. She knew now that he loved her as much as she loved him.

Once Baptista had said to her, 'When he trusts you with his deepest secret, you will know he truly loves you.'

Last night he'd trusted her like that, enough to tell of the one fury above all others that tortured him, his feelings of guilt that he had inadvertently caused the death of his parents. And from that everything followed, including his refusal to be part of the family, or to accept more from them than the bare minimum. He felt he had no right.

But now they could confront the horrors together. She might even manage to show him that a child's feeling of guilt should be put in the past, and not allowed to haunt the man.

She stretched luxuriously, feeling every inch of her body enjoy the sensation of being newly alive. Such love! And it was hers to enjoy for the rest of her life in ever deepening happiness.

She checked quickly to see if he'd left her a note on the pillow, but he hadn't. It wouldn't have been like him, she thought. No frills, just an honest man.

She bounded out of bed and got quickly under the shower, emerging bright eyed and refreshed, and hurried into the kitchen. And it was there that she saw the note, leaning against the kettle.

It said simply,

My dear, I came closer to you than to anyone in my life before, but perhaps, for me, that was too close.
I'm not fit to love and be loved. I only know how to give pain.
Forgive me and, for both our sakes, go back to England.

Bernardo.

She had to read it again and again to take it in. The sheer brutal simplicity of the short message was like being pounded by hammers. The man who'd loved her with such passion and tenderness in the night had fled her in the dawn, like an evil thing that he must escape to survive.

And now she heard what she'd blotted out before, Bernardo's anguished voice begging her not to force the unbearable truth from him.

'It was my own fault,' she whispered. 'I made him tell me. He wasn't ready, but I forced it out of him. I had everything, and I threw it away. Oh God, how could I be so stupid?'

Suddenly the pride that had sustained her broke. Until this moment she'd won every round, and done so with such deceptive ease that she'd thought that was all there was to it. Now she saw how she'd thrown it all away, and she must stop that happening, no matter what she had to do.

She huddled on some clothes and ran out into the street. Stumbling, slipping, grasping the wall, she made her way blindly up the street to Bernardo's house near the top. There was the little alley between the shops that led to his door. Gasping, she made her way along it, blinking in the poor light and finding the door by feel.

'Bernardo!' she screamed. *'Bernardo!'*

The door was opened at once. Stella stood there in tears.

'He's gone,' she said. 'An hour ago.' She looked at Angie with sympathy. She had always understood the position, and been rooting for them.

'Didn't he say where?' Angie begged.

'Sometimes he goes away like this. He never says where.'

'But when will he come back?'

Stella's shrug was eloquent. 'He'll come back when he comes back.'

'No, wait—' Angie was trying to pull herself together, inwardly saying keep calm, don't panic. 'This place is snowed in.'

'He spoke of his car,' Stella said unhappily.

Angie counted every step down to the great gate that led out of Montedoro. Once there she could see the marks left in the snow. There were her own footsteps from when she'd gone down to fetch Bernardo, then two sets of steps overlapping, when they'd climbed back up together.

And there was another set, firmly heading down the hill, leaving sharp, emphatic imprints in the brilliant morning light. Angie strained her eyes against that cruel light, looking for any sign of the steps turning to come back.

But they went on down until they vanished into the mist.

CHAPTER TEN

SOON the news of Heather's pregnancy had spread through the whole family, to general rejoicing. When the snow cleared Angie drove down to Palermo and was received with open arms by Heather and Baptista. The three women settled down to a pleasant afternoon together.

It was almost incredible how different everything felt on the coast. Here there was rain but no snow, the air was almost warm enough for spring, and there was even a glimmer of sunshine. But she had chosen a man from the mountains, and despite the harshness, even, it seemed, the cruelty of that life, she wasn't ready yet to give up on her choice.

As she had cakes and coffee with Heather and Baptista she was uncomfortably conscious of the question they were both refusing to ask. They knew Bernardo had battled through atrocious weather to return to her, and they were surprised that he hadn't come down with her now. But she had her defence mechanisms in place, carefully rehearsed to sound natural.

'If you two could see yourselves,' she chuckled. 'Your ears are flapping.'

'So tell us,' Heather demanded, 'then they won't need to flap.'

'So nothing. He came back. We had a meal together. It's all very friendly and civilised. Now he's away for a few days. Baptista, that cake is delicious. Can I have some more?'

'It's crawling with calories,' Heather said darkly. 'You'll get fat—I wish.'

'Not as fast as you will,' Angie teased, skilfully turning the conversation back to Heather's pregnancy.

Luckily they both accepted this and asked no more questions. Angie didn't feel up to telling them how Bernardo had vanished while she was still ecstatic from his loving, and driven off, apparently into oblivion.

She'd had hours since then to ponder what he'd told her about the feeling of guilt that still tormented him from his childhood. Now she looked at Baptista and wondered if his foster mother really would hate him if she knew the truth. Somehow Angie couldn't imagine it of that great and generous woman, but how would she react to the discovery that her husband had died needlessly?

Once Baptista had said, 'I can only guess at his deepest secret, and I may be wrong.' For a fleeting moment Angie was tempted to speak out, but then she knew she mustn't. Bernardo had spoken to her in confidence and then regretted it so fiercely that he'd fled, rejecting her and their love with heart breaking finality. She had no right to repeat anything he'd said, even to Baptista.

After a while they were joined by a tall, white-haired man who turned out to be Federico, the 'old friend' from the party.

'He's more than that,' Heather murmured into her ear. 'Years and years ago he and Baptista were in love with each other. She calls him Fede. Now he comes almost every day and they sit holding hands. It's so sweet to see them together.'

It was true, Angie thought, watching the two old people, so happy in each other's company. They had been lovers once, and they were lovers still, although differently. Somehow Bernardo had missed the truth about

them. But then, Angie reflected sadly, Bernardo wasn't
very perceptive about people.

She had a pleasant surprise with the arrival of the brothers. Renato had altered. His joy in his wife was quiet but
so heartfelt, and his attitude to her so tender that Angie
finally began to like him.

Lorenzo too had changed, although it was harder for
her to be sure just how. He was still the merry hearted
charmer that nature had made him, but he seemed to have
mysteriously grown in confidence, and Angie sensed it
had something to do with Renato's happiness. Lorenzo's
love for his older brother had once been tinged with awe
but now there was a subtle change in the power balance
between them. Lorenzo had held the happiness of three
people in his hands, and by doing the right thing he'd
saved them all. Now Renato had acknowledged it and
nothing would ever be the same between them again.

He greeted Angie with a brotherly kiss, as though she
was already a member of the family, and, sitting down,
began to tell her about the trip he was about to take to
the States.

'New York, New Orleans, Los Angeles, Chicago—
spreading the Martelli word wherever I go.'

'Yes, well, I heard you daren't show your face in
Britain again,' Angie teased.

'That was a misunderstanding,' he said loftily. 'The
magistrate fined me, I paid it—'

'And high-tailed it out of the country while the going
was good.'

'My big sister's been opening her big mouth,' Lorenzo
said with a good natured grin at Heather.

She heard him, and returned the smile. So did Renato.
They were sitting together, the picture of blissful contentment, bathed in their own happiness and the happiness

they had brought to others. This was the Martelli family at its best, Angie thought, and in the same moment came the realisation that this was the family Bernardo had rejected as he had rejected her. Because something in him made it easier to reject warmth and loving kindness than to accept it. After the other night she partly understood what that 'something' was, and her heart ached that he wouldn't turn to her, seeking help and consolation in her love.

As soon as it was polite to do so she left the Residenza and drove home to the mountains, which had never seemed so lonely.

Lorenzo was in the States for two months, sending back a stream of big orders and covering himself with glory. He returned in the second week of April, and one of the first things he did was to visit Angie, arriving just as she was finishing evening surgery.

'You're welcome to stay if you don't mind something microwaved,' she said.

'Sounds fine.'

From her freezer he selected a vegetarian lasagne and she put it in the oven.

'No wine for me,' she said as he produced a bottle. 'Pour me an orange juice.' While he did so she laid the table, glad to have company. 'I want to hear all about America,' she said.

Instead of answering, Lorenzo grinned in a way that made Angie raise her eyebrows. 'What's her name?' she demanded at once.

'I don't know why you women always jump to one conclusion. I spent some time with the daughter of family friends in New York. Her name's Helen, and before you start listening for wedding bells, I'm the last man in the world she'd dream of marrying. She told me that in the first ten minutes.'

'You proposed to her in ten minutes?'

'She didn't wait for a proposal. She just rushed to tell me not to bother.'

'You don't mean you've met a woman who's immune to your charm?'

'If you like to put it that way,' he said, slightly piqued.

'Well, don't keep me in suspense. Tell me—*ouch!*'

A fork had fallen to the floor and jabbed her foot. Leaning down for it, she found the flagstones swimming.

'Are you all right?' Lorenzo asked in alarm. He rushed across the floor and took her shoulders, steadying her as he raised her.

'Yes, I'm fine,' she said quickly.

'You look a bit peaky.'

'It's been a long, hard day. I didn't have time for lunch, and that's fatal.'

'Well, you sit there and I'll finish. Even I can cook with a microwave.'

He was as good as his word, serving her with a comical flourish that made her laugh.

'If you were hoping to see Bernardo, he still isn't here,' she said as they were eating.

'I know. Mamma told me he was still off somewhere. It's you I came to see. How are you managing?'

'Better than anyone expected.'

'You mean better than *he* expected.'

'Yes, I suppose so.' She gave a brittle laugh. 'I keep wishing he'd come back so that I can say, "I told you so".'

'He used to do this a lot when we were boys, you know. It's not enough for him to live in the same world as the rest of us. He has to have another one, all his own, where he makes the rules and nobody else is invited. And some-times he has to vanish into it. But it's hard on you. What's the point of your coming here to be with him, if *he* isn't here?'

'I didn't come here to be with him,' Angie said stonily. 'I came to teach him a lesson.' Her voice broke. 'I seem to have rather overdone it.'

'Don't say that.' Lorenzo took both of her hands in his, and his voice was kind. 'It isn't your fault. My brother's a fool. Well, we all are, but Bernardo's a different kind of fool. Renato schemes and connives, and sometimes he makes a mess of things by being too clever for his own good. Me, I'm just a plain, straightforward idiot. But Bernardo's thoughts are all dark and tangled up so that he can't see what's staring him in the face.'

There was such kindness in his eyes that she thought wistfully how different things might have been. How nice it would be to have Lorenzo as a brother! The temptation to confide in him was overwhelming. She might have yielded to it if the doorbell hadn't rung. A moment later Ginetta ushered a sharp-faced young man into the room.

'Not you again!' Angie said, with a loathing that made Lorenzo stare at her.

The man was in his late twenties with lean features and a supercilious stare. His manner suggested a barely sup-pressed impatience. Angie introduced him as Carlo Bondini, but she did so briefly and without warmth, add-ing, 'Signor Bondini, I asked you not to bother me again.'

'I merely thought you might have changed your mind, on reflection.'

'Well, I haven't.'

'I can increase my offer by another ten million lire. It's a very good offer.'

'It would be an excellent offer if I wanted to sell, but I don't. Why can't you take no for an answer?'

'Because this is exactly the kind of practice I'm looking for.'

'Then please keep looking and find another one. And don't come back.'

'Oh, I'll be back.'

'No, you've been told not to,' Lorenzo said with deceptive affability. 'But you never could take a hint. I've just remembered you. We were at school together. I didn't like you then, either. Get going and keep going.'

Bondini looked as if he might dispute the point, but he wasn't built for heroics against a man of Lorenzo's size, and he wisely decided to let the matter drop.

'We'll leave it there for the moment,' he said with a shrug. 'But don't reject my offer without careful thought.' His eyes on Angie were like gimlets. 'You don't have that much time, after all. I'm a doctor, too, remember, and I have eyes—*signorina*.'

He made the last word an insult. Then he was gone.

'Does he pester you often?' Lorenzo exploded.

'He turns up every two weeks with an improved offer.'

'But why? What's so marvellous about this—? I mean—'

'Did you really know him at school?'

'Yes. I used to get him to do my homework for me,' Lorenzo confessed with a grin that wasn't in the least ashamed.

'I thought you didn't like him.'

'The transaction was purely commercial. I wonder where he's suddenly getting money from.'

'Can't you guess?' Angie asked with a sigh. 'Bernardo, of course. He's trying to buy me out.'

'But you can't—I mean—not now—not if I understood him correctly—'

'I expect you did,' Angie said with a wan smile.

'That settles it,' Lorenzo said with sudden resolution. 'Now it's a family matter.'

The farmhouse stood at the end of a dirt track, most of which was hidden by trees. It had been abandoned long ago, although the building had been roughly patched up to make it habitable if not comfortable.

Bernardo saw his brother coming from a distance and was waiting by the door, his face dark and unwelcoming. 'How the devil did you find this place?'

'I've always known about it,' Lorenzo told him. 'You used to slip away up here when we were boys, and once I followed you. You never knew.'

'If I had I'd have found somewhere else.'

'I know. That's why I didn't tell you. I knew your odd ways. We all did.'

Bernardo reluctantly stood aside to let him enter. 'Is it odd to want a little privacy?'

'Not privacy. Isolation. *Maria vergine!* How do you live in this place?'

'Very well when I'm left alone.'

'Look I don't know what went wrong between you and Angie, but I'm willing to bet it was your fault. You've got a beautiful, brilliant woman in love with you, so of course you weren't happy until you'd rejected her, the way you've rejected us all for years. But I'm still your brother and I'm not going to let you screw up the best thing that ever happened to you.'

Bernardo didn't answer, only stared at him with bleak, anguished eyes.

Lorenzo said more gently, 'The world won't go away,

Bernardo. It's out there and it's full of unpleasant people, like Carlo Bondini.'

'What do you know about him?' Bernardo demanded sharply.

'I saw his last visit, and I came to tell you to get him off Angie's back. He's trying to bully her.'

Bernardo swore. 'I told him to offer for the practice. I never meant him to upset her.'

'You should choose your instruments more carefully. If you ever let your brothers past the guarded gates I could have told you he's a nasty piece of work.'

'I can do without your advice,' Bernardo said coldly. 'Ever since Renato acknowledged a debt to you you've become damned insufferable.'

'I was always insufferable,' Lorenzo remarked with perfect truth. 'But that's not the point. Things have changed. Something's going on. I'm not sure what. I have my suspicions but I'm not a doctor—unlike Bondini, as he was careful to point out.'

'What are you saying?' Bernardo asked slowly.

'I'm saying that if you're going to add to the family, it's about time you started being a member of it.'

The way back was like driving through a tunnel of blossoms. The most fertile land on earth was flaunting its lush beauty in the sun, and everywhere Bernardo looked there was harmony that seemed to invite him on.

Until he saw the path ahead.

By stepping on the accelerator he was there in a couple of seconds, too fast for the crowd of young men to disperse from where they had been surrounding the woman on the mule. They were all smiling but in a way that suggested menace, and one was holding the mule's bridle.

At the sound of Bernardo's car they looked up in alarm, and scattered.

He didn't bother pursuing. He saw only the woman and the thunderstruck look she was giving him.

'So you came back?' Angie said distantly. 'I suppose I should thank you for getting rid of them. Well, thank you. But now I'd like to go.'

'What are you doing in this place?'

'Visiting my patients.'

'On your own? Are you mad?'

'I never had trouble before.'

'So why suddenly now?'

Her face set against him. 'How should I know?'

'I think you do.'

'And I think I'd like you to just fade away and let me get on. I have two more people to see.'

'Then get into my car.'

'And what about Jason?'

'Who?'

'Antonio needs Nesta on the farm now, so I bought my own mule. We can't put him in the car.'

'He can walk behind. Please get in.' He reached up to grasp her wrist, but was almost blown back by the freezing look in her eyes.

'Take your hands off me at once, Bernardo, and never dare to do that again.'

'You can't go on alone,' he said emphatically.

'Then you can drive behind me. But please stay where I don't have to look at you.'

He had no choice but to do it her way. Moving at her pace he had time to notice the interest she aroused, the workers who stopped in the fields to watch her pass, but without the friendly greetings they would once have given her. There was something eerie about their silent curiosity.

In the first house she went to it was much the same. Her patient was a very old woman, desperately ill and moving towards the end of her life. Thanks to Angie she was doing so peacefully and mostly without pain. Her family were grateful and showed it by treating the doctor with courtesy, but their manner was shadowed by reserve. Bernardo's appearance evidently surprised them, making them nudge each other and exchange significant looks.

The second visit was to a young couple where the wife was having a difficult pregnancy. They were worried because their first child had been born with a facial deformity. Bernardo had seen the little girl once, for her parents kept her hidden and at six years old she was very shy. But she ran out as soon as Angie arrived, bouncing with excitement and evidently considering her a friend.

When Angie was packing her bag a strange thing happened. The wife suddenly threw her arms about her and gave her a big hug. Then she drew back and smiled into her face.

'*Amicu,*' she said. Friend.

There was a touch of defiance in her manner, as though she felt the need to declare her friendship before a critical world.

'Where have you left your car?' Bernardo asked as they left the house.

'It's at home. For trips like this I take Jason all the way. Benito stables him for me with his own mules.'

'And what about the danger?'

'There's never been any danger.'

'Don't tell me those lads weren't threatening you.'

'Not openly, but they weren't being nice.'

'Right. I'm coming home with you, and we have to talk.'

'I don't think so.'

He ground his teeth. 'Have supper with me.'

'No, thank you.'

'Then I'll come to you.'

'I haven't invited you to supper. Good day to you, *signore*.'

She hopped nimbly onto Jason's back and trotted away. Bernardo cursed but he didn't make the mistake of following her.

Two patients to go, she thought as she neared the end of evening surgery. Her back was aching and she was tired after the heavy day. Not long now, then she could put her feet up.

But when she looked out into the waiting room she found another presence. Bernardo glanced up and met her eyes, his own challenging, telling her she couldn't avoid him.

At last she waved off the last patient and locked her door, knowing that she couldn't avoid this confrontation any longer. She would have liked to put it off because she didn't know what she was going to say to him. When he'd appeared out of nowhere that afternoon her heart had leapt unreasonably. But she'd controlled her momentary joy, telling herself it meant nothing. She was simply relieved that he'd come to rescue her. Apart from that, she was hollow inside. That was what she tried to believe.

And now here he was, looking so exactly as she'd pictured him that it was as though her anguished dreams had come to life. For two months she'd battled against despair, one moment hardening her heart against him, the next moment telling herself not to become hard because she couldn't afford to.

There were the nights when she'd cried herself to sleep, and the nights when she'd slept like a stone from the

moment her head touched the pillow, because she'd
worked herself into the ground. But no matter how long
or how deeply she slept she always awoke feeling as
though she'd been dredged up from the bottom of a deep
pit. She grew so used to waking up feeling bad that at
first she missed the signs that matters had changed irrev-
ocably.

It was almost comical, she thought without amusement.
She, a doctor, to be caught so easily. Seduced and abandoned like some idiotic Victorian maiden without knowledge or common sense.

And now he was here, and she didn't know what she
wanted to say to him.

'Are you all right?' he asked quietly.

'Yes, everything's fine with me. Can I offer you some
coffee?' She went into the kitchen without waiting for his
answer. 'And something to eat?' She was looking in her
freezer.

'No, thank you.'

'It's no trouble.' She was still rummaging, not looking
at him.

'Will you leave that for a moment and talk to me?' he
demanded.

'Talking to you is dangerous, Bernardo. We talked two
months ago, remember?'

He drew a sharp breath. 'I went because I couldn't bear
to stay.'

'Thank you!'

'You don't understand—perhaps I was wrong to go, but
it seemed the best for both of us.'

'And so you sent Bondini to buy me out.'

'Lorenzo told me how he behaved. I never meant him
to bully you. I've seen him since and made him sorry. He
won't be back.'

He waited for her to answer but she was busy with supper.

'Lorenzo told me something else too,' he said at last.

'Lorenzo seems to have been busy.'

'He's my—my brother. He cares about us.'

'Yes,' she said in a softened voice. 'He came to see how I was, and then he got word to you. He's a kind man.' She glanced up suddenly, taking him by surprise. 'Not like you.'

'You know what I am,' he said harshly. 'I'm a devil. I can't help myself. You should have avoided me when you had the chance. But you can't avoid me now.'

'Now? What's so different about now, Bernardo?'

'You mean—you're not—?'

'Pregnant? Yes, I am. I'm carrying your child. But nothing's changed.' She faced him. 'Do you understand that? Nothing.'

CHAPTER ELEVEN

'NOTHING'S changed,' she repeated when he didn't answer.

'You can't say that,' he said flatly. 'Everything has changed.'

She tried to turn away but he took hold of her shoulders and kept her facing him. Even with such slight contact, the remembered feel of her body unnerved him, and he kept his hands there, sensing her warmth through her shirt. If she'd shown the slightest sign of softening he would have drawn her into his arms and kissed her ardently. And then, even he, who was uneasy with words, would have tried to tell her of the bittersweet happiness that had possessed him ever since he'd suspected that she was to bear his child. He was an old-fashioned man and, above all, a Sicilian. To create a child with the beloved woman was a joy that wiped out all else, making old fears and torments at least manageable. He couldn't have expressed these things, but he would have done his awkward best if he'd seen anything in her face to encourage him. But there was nothing, and his heart sank.

'Everything has changed,' he repeated, like a man trying to convince himself.

The buzzer on the microwave sounded, and she drew away from him. 'Well, one thing has altered,' she conceded. 'The people here don't know what to make of me any more. They got used to my foreign tongue and my new-fangled ways and they closed their eyes to my reprehensible trousers. But now,' she added lightly, 'I think a few of them feel I may have gone just a little too far.'

It was when she talked like this that he felt all at sea. Colourful dramatics he could have coped with, but ironic English understatement left him floundering. Only one thing got through to him with the force of a punch in the stomach. She, not he, was master of this situation.

'Are they treating you badly?' he asked, recalling the curious looks she'd received that afternoon.

'Not really. I'm not showing yet and they're not certain. But they look at me and wonder.'

'But how did the rumour start at all, so soon?'

'Mother Francesca knows, and Sister Elvira came in suddenly last week, while we were talking. I remembered afterwards that Sister Elvira is a cousin of Nico Sartone.'

'That explains everything.'

'Yes, he must be thrilled to have a weapon against me at last. I could strangle that man. He doesn't care whom he hurts as long as he can get back at me. People who need my help are slowly becoming nervous of asking for it in case their neighbours disapprove. Not all of them, though. He thought he could turn the whole town against me, and he was wrong.'

'Yes, it'll be a pleasure to wipe the smile off his face,' Bernardo growled.

'How are you going to do that?'

He frowned. '*We* are going to do it.'

'How?'

'Isn't it obvious?'

'Not to me,' Angie said stubbornly.

He stared at her. 'The sooner our marriage takes place the better.'

There. It had happened. He wanted to marry her. But there was no surge of gladness such as should have blessed this moment. Instead, the other self—the awkward one who had to make everything difficult, and whom Bernardo could evoke in her with fatal ease—became not merely indignant but stubborn. Just who did he think he was?

'Us? Get married?' she echoed, as though experimenting with a new language. 'Why would we do that?'

He was floundering again. Angie's eyes were full of a cool, faintly hostile, appraisal that baffled him. 'Because we are having a baby,' he said.

'*We're* not doing anything. *I'm* having a baby. Oh, you fathered it biologically, but no part of it has been yours since you upped and left the next morning, without a word.'

'I was wrong to do that, and I'm sorry. I should have thought of this—I suppose I just assumed that, since you were a doctor—'

'Stop! Don't say any more. You're making it worse with every word. You blame yourself for not thinking I might get pregnant, but not for the way you hurt me. Have you any idea what it did to me to wake and find you gone? And that charming little note—"little" being the operative word. Was that really all I deserved?'

He reddened. 'I'm not good with words—'

'You're all right with words, Bernardo. It's feelings you're no good at. You wouldn't marry me for love, but now I'm a brood mare, that's different, isn't it?'

He tore his hair. 'All I meant was—your pregnancy seems to solve the problems.'

She regarded him in pity. 'I said you were no good with feelings and you've just proved it. If I married you for such a reason our problems would just be beginning. I would gladly have married you for love, but I don't want a man who feels I contrived a child to trap him. Without love, the deal's off.'

The bitter words seemed to be coming out of their own accord. Part of her longed to bite them back and fall into his arms. He wanted to marry her. No matter how it had come about, wouldn't a sensible woman take what she could and build on it?

But the 'other' Angie wasn't a sensible woman. She was an awkward, prickly, troublesome creature who reacted like a hedgehog when her pride was affronted. She was the one who'd jumped at Baptista's suggestion of coming out here, and she wouldn't be banished back into her box now she'd served her purpose.

So now she was the one who regarded Bernardo out of furious eyes and said, 'Marry you? What do you think I am?'

'I don't understand anything you say. You've won, isn't that enough?'

'No, it's not enough. We're further apart now than before you mentioned marriage because if you think I've "won" then you believe you've lost. I didn't even realise we were fighting. I thought we were trying to find the way to each other. And that night—' her voice shook as memories came back to her, but she controlled it and kept her distance '—after that night, it almost seemed as if we'd found the way. You told me what was troubling you. All right, maybe I pushed too hard, but you might have trusted my love.

'But I forgot, you can't cope with someone who loves you because it means coming close.' Tears were sliding down her cheeks, but she ignored them, speaking softly and with heartbreak. 'You've spent the last twenty years rejecting anyone who tried to get near you, and now you can't see a pair of open arms without turning your back.

So go ahead, turn it again. My arms aren't even open any more, *because there's no point.*'

'You don't really mean that,' he said quietly.

'You think not? Why shouldn't I? Remember what you said in your note? "I only know how to give pain." It was true, but I was too stupid to realise it. We should have stayed strangers.'

'We can never be strangers again,' he said quietly.

'Why, because I'm having your child?'

'Not only that. Because of things we can't forget. I've tried to forget them, tried night after night to blot out everything you are to me, but I can't do it. If this hadn't happened I was coming back anyway to beg your forgiveness and ask to start again.'

'Words,' she said with a sigh.

'Meaning that you don't believe me?'

'I don't know,' she said huskily. 'I only know that it's too late for words. I once wanted to marry you so much. Now I know that marrying you would be fatal. Please Bernardo, just go away.'

'I'll go, but it isn't final. Nothing has been settled tonight. I won't give you up so easily.'

She watched as he went to the door and gave her one look before departing. She dried her tears and found that she was simply too tired to feel anything. The emotions they'd shared that night should have wrung her out, but they didn't because she was already wrung out. All she could think of was getting to bed, going to sleep, and not having to think or feel anything, ever again.

She knew now that the problems she faced with the town would get worse, and they did. There wasn't a soul in Montedoro who didn't know that Bernardo was the father of her child, but they'd suspended judgement until he returned.

'They were so sure he was going to "make an honest woman" of me,' Angie said bitterly to Heather, who came to call, full of concern.

'You mean he isn't?'

'Oh, he wants to. It's me that won't make an honest man of him.'

'You two have got yourself in a pickle, haven't you? It's the sort of situation that needs Baptista to sort it out, like she did for me.' Heather patted her own pregnancy bump. She was three months ahead of Angie, who didn't show at all as yet.

'I don't think even Baptista could do much with this situation,' Angie said wryly.

'Not unless Bernardo asked her,' Heather agreed. 'And he won't do that. You know what he's like.'

As the town realised that Bernardo's return didn't herald an immediate marriage they began to look uneasily at Angie. She was too popular to be totally condemned, but now nobody knew what to make of her. Bernardo had said he wasn't giving up, but he too seemed to keep his distance, until the night she returned late from being called out, and found him leaning against her front door. Too tired to argue, she let him in.

'Where is Ginetta?' he asked, looking around at the empty house.

'Her mother forced her to stop working for me.'

He remembered suddenly how his mother's servants had all been middle-aged. No mother would let her daughter work for the town *prostituta*.

'Then you should have got a replacement,' he said. 'It's too much for you to do all on your own.'

'I'm not alone. One or two of the nuns drop in to help me. They've been wonderful. But some of the others—'

he thought she sighed a little '—won't come near me now.'

'We are not like other people,' Marta had said to her son. *'We are set apart because of your father. There are those in this town who will never come near me. You— yes. Me—no.'*

Now he tried to remember if anyone had shunned him as an unmarried father, and he couldn't. It was she who was shunned, even if not wholly, because these people knew that they needed her. They would take from her, but not give to her. Rage consumed him, and it made him cruel.

'Why should that worry you?' he asked coldly. 'You don't depend on this for your bread.'

He was ashamed before the words were out of his mouth. A sick, weary look washed over her face as she said, 'That's true.'

'Forgive me,' he said gently. When she didn't answer he went on his knees beside her and took her hands. 'Forgive me. I should never have spoken to you like that.'

She smiled, but he knew she was still withdrawn from him. 'I'll make you something to eat,' he said.

'I don't really—'

'You will eat it,' he said firmly. 'You must keep up your strength. And perhaps—' he laid his hand briefly on her shoulder '—perhaps you will also do it to please me.'

In another moment she would have rested her cheek on his hand, but it was gone before she could move.

She heard dishes clattering in her little kitchen and soon delicious smells began to waft towards her. Of course Bernardo could cook, she thought. It was all part of his determination to need nobody else. Right now she was glad of it.

She began to remove her outdoor clothes, and he was

there at once, taking them from her and hanging them up. He neither smiled nor uttered pleasant words, but his hands were as gentle as they were firm. When they were finished he said, 'Sit down.'

'Let me lay the table.'

'*I* will lay the table. *You* will do as you are told.'

It was blissful to be waited on. She sat in sleepy content while he spread the checked cloth on the little table, set out knives and forks, salt, pepper, plates and wine glasses.

'No wine for me,' Angie said. 'Not while I'm pregnant.'

'What do you drink?'

'Tea. You'll find it in the container over there.'

He served up pasta with sardines, which she found delicious. He ate with her but actually consumed very little as his eyes were mostly on her, to ensure that she ate every mouthful. When he wasn't watching her he was darting to the stove to oversee the cooking of the meatballs for the next dish. And he made the tea.

It was horrible. Bernardo had never made tea before and it showed.

'What did I do wrong?' he asked, seeing her face.

'I don't think the water boiled.'

'I'll make it again.'

Despite her protests he insisted on doing so, scowling until he got it right. She surveyed him tenderly, feeling a little ache in her heart. He was so inexpressibly dear, so close, so distant.

'That's good,' she said at last, smiling as she sipped the tea.

'Like the English make it?' he demanded suspiciously.

'Like I make it. Well—almost.'

They both smiled. For a brief instant the barriers were down.

'Angie—'

The scream of the doorbell made him drop the hand
he'd reached out to her. Cursing under his breath he strode
to the door.

'What are you doing here?' he demanded of Nico
Sartone.

'A small matter of a prescription the doctor promised
me,' Sartone said, smiling horribly and oiling his way into
the room. 'Signore Farani needs his ointment tonight, doctor, and you were going to send the prescription down to
me—'

'Oh, yes, I'm sorry, it slipped my mind,' Angie said
tiredly. 'Just a moment.'

'Couldn't you have reminded her tomorrow?' Bernardo
snapped.

'But the ointment is needed tonight,' Sartone said with
the same smile. His eyes, like lizard's, darted around the
room.

'Then you could have given it to him tonight and sorted
the paperwork tomorrow,' Bernardo pointed out, keeping
his temper with difficulty.

'Give a controlled drug without a prescription?' Sartone
echoed in horror.

'It's an eczema ointment for a man you've known for
years,' Bernardo said with suppressed rage. 'A few hours
wouldn't have hurt, and don't tell me you haven't done
this a hundred times before because I know you have.'

'Only with Dr Fortuno,' Sartone said, still smiling.
'Alas, we all got into some very unfortunate habits with
him, but the new doctor, as we all know, has much higher
standards, to which we all aspire.'

'Here's the prescription,' Angie said, coming back
quickly. 'And please give my apologies to Signor Farani.'

'Yes, I'm afraid he isn't too pleased with you,' Sartone said with poisonous sweetness.

'Get out,' Bernardo told him softly. 'Get out now, while you're safe.'

Sartone's reptile eyes flickered between them and his smile grew more sickly. 'Ah, then perhaps we can soon expect an interesting announce—'

'Goodnight, *signore*,' Angie said firmly before Bernardo could speak.

He knew when he'd pushed his luck to the limit, and slithered out hastily.

'Perhaps you should go too,' Angie said.

'Must I? I thought—'

'It was nice of you to cook for me, but I'd like to go to bed now.'

He thought of the moment of warmth and laughter when they'd been interrupted, and knew, with a sigh, that it was too late to go back to that. Whatever might have sprung from that moment wouldn't happen now.

'Yes, of course, you need your rest.' He hesitated, then dropped a brief kiss on her cheek. She gave him a half smile, but no other sign of encouragement, and he picked up his coat and left.

As soon as Bernardo entered his shop Sartone became occupied with something that took his whole attention. But nothing budged Bernardo who stood there, silent and implacable, waiting until the shop was empty.

'Now, look,' Sartone said at last, 'I don't want any trouble.'

'And I don't want to see any more exhibitions of your spite to an excellent doctor who's doing wonders for this community. Don't pretend that last night was an accident.'

'Whatever it was, it's surely between the doctor and myself?'

'Do you think I'll stand by and see you persecute her? Are you hoping to run her out? Think again.'

Sartone gave a titter that made Bernardo clench and unclench his hands. 'I don't think it'll be necessary for me to do anything. Unless you do your duty, time is hardly on the lady's side, is it?'

Bernardo got out of the shop as fast as he could before he committed murder. In the street outside he almost collided with Father Franco and Mayor Donati. He straightened himself, and them, and stood there muttering fiercely.

'I know better curses than that,' Father Marco said wisely.

'True Sicilian curses for all situations,' the mayor confirmed.

'There are no Sicilian curses for this situation,' Bernardo growled.

'Why?' they demanded with one voice.

Before he could answer Sartone came out of the shop, driven by hate, and moving too fast to check himself at the last minute.

'You ought to think of my words,' he shrilled. 'She can't afford to drive customers away, because soon she won't have any. *Prostituta.*'

There was a scream from a woman nearby. The next moment Sartone was lying on the cobbles with three men standing over him.

Nobody had seen which one of them had knocked him down.

Baptista was enjoying a late night cup of tea with Heather and Renato when her unexpected visitor was announced, but one glance at Bernardo's face was enough to make her shoo the other two kindly away. He looked, as she afterwards told the others, like a man ascending the scaffold.

But when they were alone he seemed unable to come to the point. After refusing offers of refreshment he paced the room uneasily, making polite enquiries after her health. At last he said abruptly,

'I'd better go. I shouldn't have intruded on you at this hour. I came too late.'

'You certainly left it very late to come to me,' Baptista said, subtly altering his words, 'but as for whether you came *too* late—why don't we find out? It may not really be too late at all.'

He paced some more.

'I had a visitor yesterday,' he said at last. 'A young girl called Ginetta. She used to work for Angie, but her mother forced her to leave when the ''scandal'' developed. She admires Angie, wants to be like her, maybe even be a doctor. She's hoping for our marriage, to change her mother's mind. I had to tell her it was unlikely. When I told her why, she couldn't believe me. She says no woman would refuse to marry the father of her child.

'She made it very clear that it was my duty to persuade Angie into marriage, ''for everyone's sake''.' He gave a grunt of laughter. 'They love her. They disapprove of her, but they admire her and they want her to stay.'

'You're reading a lot into the words of one young girl.'

'That was just yesterday. Today I had a full scale deputation, the priest, the mayor, the Reverend Mother, all wanting to tell me my duty. When I pointed out that the refusal came from her, Olivero Donati had the nerve to tell me to look into my heart and ask what I'd done to make ''this fine woman'' refuse me. Father Franco backed

him up, which I'll swear is the only time in history those
two have agreed on anything.

'The whole town is looking to me to put matters right,
and I can't convince them that it doesn't lie with me.'

'Perhaps it does,' Baptista said thoughtfully. 'Maybe
you just haven't found the right way.'

'There isn't a right way,' Bernardo said at once. 'I
know I was wrong to leave like that, but I thought she'd
be better off without me.'

'Well, now she seems to agree with you,' Baptista observed dryly.

Bernardo checked himself in his pacing.

'I'm lying,' he said with an effort. 'I was thinking of
myself when I left. I told her such things—I let her come
so close—I was afraid—'

Baptista nodded. 'The closeness of love can be terri-
fying,' she said. 'That's why it takes so much courage.
Some people feel safer at a distance, but Angie will never
let you keep that distance. She's warm and open-hearted,
and very brave. She'll give everything and want everything in return, and if you can't give it—well, perhaps it's
best to discover these things now.'

Bernardo looked at her, aghast. 'What are you saying?'
he demanded hoarsely.

'That perhaps she really would be better off without
you.'

'Even if I love her—if she loves me—?'

Baptista spoke thoughtfully. 'Sometimes love—even
great love—isn't enough.'

'I don't—believe that,' he said with difficulty. He
looked at Baptista with desperate eyes. 'I don't know what
to do. *For pity's sake, help me.*'

CHAPTER TWELVE

SPRING was turning into summer, and tourists were converging on Montedoro, although few of them found their way into the side street where Angie lived, and at night it was so quiet that every footstep was noticeable.

They were strange days when she seemed to be living in limbo and several times she looked out onto the valley to see the golden eagle wheeling and swooping eerily close to her. And then one memorable day the bird turned his head, seeming to look straight into her eyes, and gave a wild scream that echoed through the mountains. Then it was gone.

To others it might have been just a scream, but to Angie, in her state of heightened sensitivity, it sounded like a shout of greeting. She had made it. She had proved herself an eagle.

And there was nobody to know or care.

She couldn't have said what awoke her in the early hours one morning, and made her go to her front door. There was nobody there, but a few lights were still on in the houses opposite. For a moment she saw a head in silhouette, turned in her direction, but it vanished at once. Then the light went off. The silence was total. It was just like any other night. Except that it wasn't. Something was very different. She stood there for a moment, listening, wondering what was happening. At last she closed the door.

The feeling of strangeness continued next day. She awoke early, feeling queasy, as she often did now, and when that passed she had a quick breakfast alone, then opened her morning surgery. But nobody came. She checked the waiting room, but it was empty. Angie was used to having fewer patients these days, but there was still a fair number who valued her skills more than her reputation, and total silence was rare. After a while she checked the waiting room again, but still there was nobody there.

Of course the weather was fine now, she told herself. Nobody was feeling poorly. But the brave words couldn't still the unease within her heart. Or the ache. She had stuck her neck out for these people, and they were abandoning her.

She looked out, but there wasn't a soul to be seen in the sunlit street. Somewhere overhead, she heard a window open, a voice went, 'Pssst!' And the window closed again.

A rumbling sound made her glance quickly to the far end of the street, just in time to see Benito and his son, both driving their painted carts across the road, before vanishing between two buildings. Which was strange, because this wasn't part of their route.

She began to wonder if she were hallucinating. At any moment she half expected someone to jump out of a trapdoor.

Giving herself a little shake Angie retreated back into her house, trying not to feel isolated. There was a pile of things to do, she told herself firmly. And she would be strong-minded, and get on with them.

But she did none of them. She stood in the middle of the floor, wondering what was happening to her.

She must be going dotty. That was it. Because otherwise, why would she imagine that she could hear a trumpet?

Back to the front door. Look out again. And this time there was no mistake. She could hear the trumpet loud and clear, and the sound of a drum, accompanying a procession that was making its way up from the bottom of the street.

She was definitely hallucinating because no way was that Baptista riding on Benito's cart at the head of the procession. But when she had closed her eyes, shaken her head and opened her eyes again the cart was still there, rumbling towards her. So was Baptista. And now Heather was sitting beside her.

Nearer they came, and now she could discern individuals walking beside the colourful cart. There was Father Marco, and beside him the mayor. On the other side of the cart walked Sister Ignatia and the Mother Superior. As everyone realised that she had seen them they all waved and smiled. They were carrying garlands and flowers, as if for a festive day, and behind them came the town band playing with huge enthusiasm and small accuracy.

As last they stopped before her house, and now she could see that the procession stretched far back down the street, encompassing so many people that she wondered if there was anyone left to run the shops.

'What—what's going on?' she asked helplessly.

Nobody spoke, but Father Marco, grinning broadly, stepped aside and revealed someone Angie hadn't noticed before.

'*Dad!*' she exclaimed. 'What are you doing here?'

'I've come to your wedding, my dear,' he said, embracing her. 'Your brothers send their love. Unfortunately they couldn't get the time off at such short notice—'

'Short notice?' she squealed. 'You announced that I'm getting married—which nobody's told *me*—and you talk about short notice? Well, I'm not getting married.'

'*Signorina*, you must,' the mayor said earnestly. 'Every one of us is here today to tell you that you must.'

'Must?' she echoed. 'What do you mean—"must"?'

There was a small commotion from the top of the street. Three men were striding towards them, Bernardo in the centre, flanked by his brothers, each dressed in their best clothes. Angie strained her eyes trying to read Bernardo's expression, but all she could see was how calm he looked, not at all like a man who'd been kidnapped.

Angie's father was helping Baptista down from the cart, then Heather, who was carrying a parcel.

'All present and correct,' Lorenzo called out merrily as the brothers came to a halt.

Angie moved closer, meeting Bernardo's eyes, her own full of suspicion. 'Did you know about this?' she demanded.

Instead of answering he threw an anguished look at Baptista. 'You promised to do the talking for me,' he growled.

'And I will,' she assured him. 'Some of the talking. But there are also things a man must say for himself.'

'It's a set-up, isn't it?' Angie asked her.

'Yes, my dear, it's a set-up. And since a lot of people have gone to a lot of trouble to set you up, the least you can do is listen to us.'

She nudged the mayor, bringing him out of the trance in which he'd been rehearsing his words. He cleared his throat and faced Angie with the air of a man determined to get it right.

'Since the day you came here you've worked hard to become one of the community,' he proclaimed, 'something which we all appreciate.'

'And I hope to continue as one of the community but—'

He mopped his brow. 'Please, *signorina*, let me get to the end.'

'Very well,' she said with an ominous calm that made him gulp.

'Er—where was I? Since the day you—oh, no—worked hard—er—'

Angie's lips twitched. 'You've done that bit.'

'Yes, yes I have, haven't I?'

'Would you like *me* to carry on?' Father Marco muttered.

'Certainly not,' Olivero said, stung. 'I am the mayor. This is my job.'

'That was never decided.'

'Pardon me, but it *was* decided.'

'It is I who will be conducting this marriage—'

'Except that you have no bride,' the little mayor pointed out with spirit. 'And if you keep interrupting you will never have a bride. And I must insist—'

Through the ensuing fracas Angie met Bernardo's eyes and saw that they were full of amusement. She pressed her lips together, trying not to laugh out loud at the antics of the two men, but mostly from sheer joy at the miracle that was happening. What you couldn't achieve for yourself, your family and friends got together to make happen for you. That was how it should be.

'*Signorina,*' the mayor said, 'I am here to tell you that if you do not settle this situation, you will be *failing in your duty* to Montedoro.'

'What do you mean, ''settle the situation''? I'm a good doctor, aren't I?'

'The best we've ever had, but—there are things—' He looked as if he wished the earth could swallow him up.

'You mean because I'm pregnant and unmarried?'

He swallowed. 'If you insist on being specific about it.'

'What about *his* duty?' she asked, indicating Bernardo.

'He's willing to do his duty,' the priest said. 'It's you that's making difficulties.'

'Shut up!' Olivero told him, incensed. 'Shut up, shut up, *shut up*!' Having found his voice, he pulled himself together and said to Angie, 'We are your friends. We love you and we want you to stay with us. But you do not yet understand this place. You don't know—as we do—that if you do not marry, sooner or later you will have to leave us, and we *will do anything* to prevent this catastrophe.'

'But it's not that simple,' Angie said, half laughing, 'There's paperwork, bureaucracy—a civil ceremony—'

'That's all been taken care of,' Baptista said with an air of triumph. 'The civil ceremony was arranged as soon as I received your birth certificate.'

'Received my birth certificate—from—?'

'Don't ask silly questions, darling,' her father said, giving her cheek a peck. 'I've been working very hard over this, and I want my full share of credit.'

Before everyone's delighted eyes he and Baptista shook hands.

'I hate to break up the love-in,' Angie said, exasperated, 'but I haven't said yes.'

'Then say it,' Lorenzo urged her, 'then we can all get on with the party.'

Bernardo came to stand before her. 'Say yes,' he begged. 'Forget my foolishness. Forget that I wasn't brave or wise enough to trust our love, until you showed me better. I didn't understand that love must be fought and struggled for, and there is nothing in the world more worth the fight. I know now and I beg you to be my wife.'

How bright the sun was, she thought, when only a moment before it had been dark. In the silence it was as though the whole world was waiting for her answer, but suddenly she couldn't speak. She could only touch his face very softly, smiling through her tears. He didn't wait for any more, but swept her into his arms. It went against the grain with this deeply private man to show his feelings in public, but he kissed her again and again in the middle of the street, while the crowd cheered and threw hats and flowers in the air.

'Hurry up,' Heather said practically. 'We've got to get you properly dressed.'

'I haven't anything suitable,' Angie protested.

'Of course not. That's why I brought you something.' Heather took one of Angie's arms, Baptista the other, and together they steered her back into the house, followed, it seemed by every woman in the village. Stella appeared, bringing Ginetta, and behind them Mother Francesca and Sister Ignatia, all beaming and full of delight at the result of their benign conspiracy.

Heather had visited a bridal hire shop in Palermo, giving them her friend's measurements, and bringing away three bridal gowns for Angie to chose from. Everyone had a say, but it was Mother Francesca, whose eye for clothes was unrivalled, who chose the soft cream silk with the tiny veil adorned with yellow roses.

As soon as this choice was made a whisper went around the women and out into the street, and a waiting child was despatched to the florist, returning a few minutes later with a bouquet of yellow roses for the bride, and ten tiny matching bouquets for the bridesmaids.

'Ten bridesmaids?' Angie echoed.

'Nobody wanted to be left out,' Sister Ignatia confided, 'but we got the number down to ten at last.'

And there were ten little girls in their Sunday best, eagerly receiving their bouquets.

'I think we have another one,' Angie said, indicating a child standing apart from the others.

It was Ella, the little girl with the deformity that she'd visited on the day Bernardo returned. Her mother moved swiftly to shield her but for once Ella struggled free of the protective arm and came to stand before Angie, touching the beautiful dress with a yearning look.

'It seems we have eleven bridesmaids,' Angie said, breaking off one of her roses and holding it out to the child. Her father, who had slipped in at that moment, stood watching the little girl.

'Are we ready to leave?' he asked, and she took his arm.

Outside the painted cart was waiting for her. When Angie and her father were aboard, with Ella wedged between them, Benito took up the reins and they began to rumble slowly over the cobbles, followed by the second cart with Baptista and Heather, and the procession falling in behind.

The first stop was the Town Hall, where it seemed they were expected. Angie was realising that the whole town was in on the plan, and her heart swelled that her friends wanted her as well as the man she loved.

She recognised people who must have come in from a distance. There was Antonio Servante, and his mother Cecilia, back on her feet now thanks to a hefty course of vitamin injections. There too was Salvatore Vitello, the one-time drunk, now a reformed character, looking sheepish and evidently having 'forgiven' her for destroying his sole claim to fame. Even Nico Sartone was present, putting a good face on it.

In the civil ceremony Mayor Donati was in his element. While the formalities were gone through he stood stiffly to attention, glaring out of the corner of his eye in case

Father Marco should put himself forward. But the priest was too wise to do what would undoubtedly have caused a riot.

Then it was over. Legally they were husband and wife, but the church service was still to come. Now Father Marco came into his own, watching the bride and groom with eagle eyes as Bernardo drew her close for a kiss.

'No hanky panky,' he cried. 'Not until you've been to church!'

'But she's already—' someone started to say without thinking, and a roar of kindly laughter went up as the anonymous caller stopped in confusion.

Angie felt Bernardo tense beside her and immediately joined in the laughter. 'Well, it's got its funny side,' she told him. 'And it's nice that our friends can share the joke.'

And she had the satisfaction of seeing him relax, then smile.

At the church Dr Wendham offered his daughter his arm for the journey down the aisle, followed by ten little bridesmaids and Ella, who insisted on walking with the bride, clutching her skirt, and resisting all attempts to remove her, until Angie said, 'She's fine as she is.'

At the altar she forgot everyone else except Bernardo, who was pale and nervous, and held onto her hand tightly as though she was all he could be sure of in a shifting world. She was in a daze. They had travelled such a rocky road and so nearly missed their destination, but here they were, each other's forever, as they were always meant to be.

The reception was held in the central piazza of Montedoro. A dozen long tables had been set up, covered with snowy white cloths that dazzled in the bright sun. Everywhere Angie looked there were flowers, some natural, some plucked from the hothouses of Federico Marcello, who sat beside Baptista, holding her hand under the table.

The speeches took a long time because everyone wanted a say, but at last it was time to cut the cake. Then the band struck up for dancing, and the bride and groom took the floor, to loud applause.

'I thought you wouldn't fit in here,' Bernardo murmured to his new wife. 'But I was so wrong. They did all this for you, to make certain that they didn't lose you.'

'Not just for me,' Angie said. 'These are your friends, your family. They did it for you. Oh, darling, don't you see? They've reached out to you. Hasn't the time come for you to reach out to them?'

He didn't answer, and she didn't press the point. It was enough that he was thinking about it.

'Did I do the right thing today?' Bernardo asked her anxiously.

She laughed and touched his face. 'Isn't it a little late to be asking me that?'

'I was desperate. No matter how I asked, you said no, but I couldn't bear to be without you. So I—forced you, I suppose.'

'I could have refused.'

'Not with the town's population standing there determined to make us tie the knot. I used to think I was a brave man, until I had to get the whole of Montedoro to do my courting for me.'

'And us,' Lorenzo put in behind him, from where he'd been shamelessly eavesdropping.

'Where would you be without your brothers?' Renato demanded as he glided by with his wife in his arms.

'And not just your brothers,' Angie said. 'I'm only guessing, but—'

'Yes, I asked Baptista's help and she gave it as freely as if I were one of her own sons.'

'Doesn't that tell you something?' she asked as they returned to their table.

'I suppose it does,' he said thoughtfully. Sitting down, he noticed her father talking to Ella with great attention, his eyes fixed on her damaged face, until her mother gave him a shy smile and took the little girl away.

Dr Wendham leaned over towards his daughter. 'I think I can do something for that child,' he said quietly.

'Yes, Dad—I'd hoped you'd be able to. I was going to ask you in my next letter,' Angie replied in a low voice.

'I'll rely on you to set it up, then. Get the X-rays done in Palermo and send them to me. It's probably best if I come over here to operate. Then I can visit you as well.'

'And you send the bill to me,' Bernardo said quickly.

Dr Wendham regarded him kindly. 'My dear boy, one of the advantages of being a rich man is that you don't have to charge people when you don't want to. Now, who shall I dance with now?'

He was gone, and a moment later they saw him leaping about on the dance floor with the mayor's wife.

Bernardo turned to Angie. 'He will really do it for nothing?'

'He does it all the time.'

His heart was in his eyes. 'I was wrong about so many things.'

'It doesn't matter, *amor mio*. We have time to put everything right. Time, and friends, and family who love us, and that's the best thing of all.'

'Yes,' he said awkwardly.

'It's your decision, but I think you should tell Baptista everything.'

'Is this the moment to take such a risk—?'

'I don't think you'll find it a risk.'

'Come with me. I can't do it without you.'

Baptista was watching them as the new husband and wife rose together, and came over to her. His body stiff with tension, Bernardo sat beside her and took Baptista's hand in his.

'How can I thank you for what you have done for me, today?' he asked gravely. 'There are no words—'

'But there is one word,' she said. 'All these years I have longed for you to accept a mother's love from me—not forgetting your true mother, but loving me also. It was a happy day when you turned to me for help. I have always loved you as my son. If only you could simply believe that.'

Bernardo's face was tortured. 'But how could I accept your love, knowing that I had no right to it? There is something—if you had known the truth all these years—'

She regarded him tenderly. 'What truth is that, my son?'

Bernardo gritted his teeth. 'That I was responsible for your husband's death. I ran away that day. I meant to come down here. I wanted to see where he lived, see his wife and his other family. I was jealous because my mother and I had to hide away. I never got here. I turned back. But in the meantime they went out to look for me in the car, and the car crashed, and they died.'

As he spoke he was forcing himself to look at Baptista's face, waiting for the revulsion to appear in it. Instead, she only gave a little smile and said, 'So that was it. Vincente couldn't imagine why you'd vanished suddenly.'

'You mean he spoke to you about it?' Bernardo asked, thunderstruck. 'But how could he? He was killed outright.'

'Yes, but before he went out searching he called me to say that he would be late home because he and your mother had to find you,' Baptista said.

'You two spoke about me?' he asked, astounded. 'You knew?'

'I knew about Vincente's second family almost from the start. I asked him about it, not blaming him, but letting him know there was no need for lies. We talked frankly, like the friends we were, and after that he was always open with me. I knew when he visited you. Oh, my dear boy, does that shock you? Did you think I had learned only after his death? Vincente and I had no secrets.'

'But you were his wife—'

'The heart has room for many kinds of love. Your mother made him so happy. It was a kind of happiness I couldn't give him, for he wasn't in love with me, any more than I was with him.' She turned fond eyes on Fede, sitting beside her. 'Another man had been my great love. Vincente knew that.

'My husband was my dearest friend, and as friends we loved each other. Once he made me promise that if anything happened to him, I would care for his other family. I gave him that promise gladly, and was proud to keep it—as far as you would let me keep it.'

Bernardo was very pale. 'When you came for me that day—I thought you hated me.'

'My dear, if you could have seen yourself—twelve years old, so certain that you were a man, determined not to cry. When I tried to take you in my arms you held yourself as stiff as a ramrod. I knew then that it was going to be hard, but I never dreamed that you would stay aloof from me all these years, refusing your father's name, and your rightful portion of your inheritance.

'I thought the time would come when we could talk.

Sadly, it never did, but in my heart I have always loved you as a mother.'

'But—I killed him,' Bernardo persisted, as though unable to believe that any good could be his.

'You were a child. Soon you will be a father. Will you blame your children all their lives for the accidents of childhood?'

Slowly Bernardo shook his head. 'No—Mamma.'

At the longed-for word, Baptista's smile was beautiful.

'If—you can forgive—' Bernardo said slowly.

'It is you who must forgive—yourself. When you've done that, you'll be ready to be a full member of this family—both you and your mother.'

'I don't understand. How can she—?'

'As you know, the Martellis have a little private chapel in the cathedral. I plan to put a plaque up to the memory of Marta Tornese. Then she too will be one of us.'

Suddenly Bernardo found that he couldn't speak. Baptista understood. Enfolding him in her arms, she met Angie's eyes and a silent message passed between them. There were still rocks ahead on his road. Probably there would always be rocks. But he had the protection of two women who loved him, and he would make it.

'Well,' Baptista said, when she had released him and wiped her eyes, while he did the same, 'it seems our family is growing bigger all the time. One wedding last year, one today, two children on the way, and—' she paused dramatically and took Fede's hand '—another wedding.'

A cheer went up. Baptista was looking at Bernardo for his reaction. She already knew that Renato and Lorenzo were glad for her, but Bernardo was the most puritanical of the three.

'Do you mean,' he asked her, 'that this is—?'

'My great love, the man I told you of. We are to be married at last.'

'As you should always have been,' Bernardo said.

'Yes,' Fede said, making one of his rare interjections, 'as we should always have been.'

'I am glad for you,' Bernardo said, shaking his hand. 'And for you, Mamma.' He kissed her. 'Recently, you've planned so many weddings for your children, it's right that you should also plan one for yourself.'

'I enjoy planning weddings,' Baptista said irrepressibly. 'And I'm certainly not finished yet.'

A silence fell. Suddenly Lorenzo became uncomfortably aware that all eyes were on him. He looked around in mounting alarm.

'Who, me?' he exclaimed. 'No way!'

'Be brave, brother,' Renato told him, his arm about Heather. 'It's not so bad when you get used to it. Ouch!' His wife had dug him in the ribs.

'Forget it,' Lorenzo said firmly. 'I'll think about it in ten years. In the meantime, no way! Do you hear me?' Alarmed, he looked at the sea of smiling faces. 'Do you hear me?'

Baptista smiled. 'Let's wait and see.'

Midnight. The guests had gone, the streets were almost empty. In the full moon a couple strolled hand in hand. They said little. They no longer needed words.

'I know nothing about people,' he said at last. 'And nothing about love, except that I feel it—for you, and for our child. I get everything wrong. You'll have to show me what to do—'

'I'm not sure that I can,' she said thoughtfully. 'I know nothing about love either. I thought I did, but that was just romance. When love came it was completely different. I found that it could be hard and cruel and made me cry with the pain of it.'

'Do you have any regrets?'

'No. It's just that I got a lot wrong, too.'

Then one of them—later, they could never remember which—said, 'We'll have to find the way together.'

EPILOGUE

BERNARDO and Angie's baby daughter was born in October, and baptised the following January, in the Martelli chapel in Palermo Cathedral. The choice was a significant one, as it marked another stage in Bernardo's reconciliation with his family. He had resumed his father's name and accepted some of his father's property, and now his choice of Palermo Cathedral over the village church in Montedoro filled Baptista with pleasure.

Not that Montedoro would miss out. Another celebration was planned there, with much gaiety, that Lorenzo was personally planning to direct.

The little chapel was crowded, as it had been for the marriage of Fede and Baptista, and the baptism of little Vincente, Renato and Heather's son.

As Angie's pregnancy advanced it became clear that she would need an assistant in the practice, but finding one was a problem. She was adamant in refusing to employ Carlo Bondini. The answer came in an unexpected way when her elder brother Steven came to visit, his face full of tragedy, seeking a refuge. He returned a week later, taking over her old house, and soon made himself so popular with the patients that they began scheming to 'imprison' him too.

It took some time to find a date for the ceremony, because Angie's father and Jack, her remaining brother, were determined to be there.

At last they were all gathered around the font in the chapel, almost directly under the recently installed plaque

185

that proclaimed Marta Tornese one of the family. Angie held her child in her arms, sometimes looking fondly down into the little girl's face, sometimes glancing up at her husband, now almost a different man. The joy of his marriage had brought him tranquillity, and now his eyes were fixed on his wife and child like a miser with treasure.

Yet he was a little troubled too. Right up to yesterday evening there had been some discussion about the names. Now he wasn't sure what had been decided, for Angie and Baptista were being secretive.

It was the moment for the godparents. As chief godmother Baptista stepped forward. The priest asked her to name the child.

'Marta,' she said, smiling at the man who was her son and not her son. 'Marta Martelli.'

What happens when you suddenly discover your happy twosome is about to be turned into a... *family?*
Do you laugh?
Do you cry?
Or...do you get married?

The answer is all of the above—and plenty more!

Share the laughter and the tears with Harlequin Romance® as these unsuspecting couples have to be

READY FOR BABY

When parenthood takes you by surprise!

THE BACHELOR'S BABY
Liz Fielding (August, #3666)

CLAIMING HIS BABY
Rebecca Winters (October, #3673)

HER HIRED HUSBAND
Renee Roszel (December, #3681)

Available wherever Harlequin books are sold.

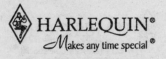
HARLEQUIN®
Makes any time special ®

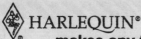